Tomboy

By

Suzana Thompson

Chapter 1

My friends were talking about hot girls, and the times when looking at those girls had been a little too hot. They all had a story to share about trying to hide their embarrassing responses in public. We were hanging out at my house and playing video games. My mom worked the night shift at a factory five and sometimes six days a week, so we freely talked about anything and everything.

"What about you, Cam?" Adam asked me before looking embarrassed when he remembered that I was a girl.

My best friend, Kyle, hooted with laughter. "Hers is probably bigger than yours."

"Shut up," Adam said. "Anyway, you haven't shared anything."

"Just saving the best for last." Kyle got a look on his face like he was remembering. "One time I hid in the girls locker room and watched the cheerleaders change clothes after practice."

Knowing him as well as I did, I kept my face expressionless while the others listened with rapt attention to this male fantasy.

"Two of them stayed behind after the other girls left. They started kissing and making out. I wanted to get a better look, so I quietly moved closer. They were so into each other that I took a chance and got even closer. I guess I made a sound, because they saw me standing there watching them. Then they asked if I wanted to join them.”

“You’re full of shit.” Adam looked angry that he had been momentarily taken in by Kyle’s story.

Everyone laughed and said rude things to Kyle. I smiled and stood up to go get a drink out of the kitchen. Hanging out with my friends was one of my favorite things in the world. It had been that way since elementary school, and it hadn’t changed in all these years. We were now in high school, but our bond was as strong as ever. I had always felt more comfortable around guys than girls. They felt comfortable around me too, as evidenced by Adam’s slip. It wasn’t the first time that one of them had forgotten that I’m a girl.

Probably the most girly thing about me was my long hair, but I had it up in a ponytail most of the time. It was an ordinary brown just like my eyes. My body was fit from playing soccer and skateboarding with my friends, but I mostly dressed like a teenage boy. I mean that literally. I bought most of my clothes in the boys department, like the shorts and t-shirt I was wearing now. My mom would shake her head and comment that she didn’t know she had given birth to twin boys. I told her that she had been right to give me a unisex name like Cameron. She had named my twin brother Connor.

He and I were close, but we had our own separate friends. His best friend, Jake, was in the kitchen when I went in to get my drink. He had five brothers and sisters, and he was the oldest child in his family. Like I said, our friends tended to gravitate toward our house for the freedom from parents. I was used to seeing Jake around at all hours. At this point there was no animosity between us. That was about to change, but I was blissfully unaware of this that Friday evening. I poured myself a glass of my favorite drink, orange juice, and turned around to see him studying me.

"I can't believe they don't see it." His blue eyes held an appraising look.

"See what? Who are they?" I asked before taking a refreshing sip of my juice.

"Your buddies out there. I can't believe they don't see *you*, Cam." His gaze was still taking me in.

Now I was really confused. "What do you mean? They see me practically every day."

He smiled in amusement like I had said something funny. "You're still a kid, aren't you? That's okay. I can wait for you to grow up."

I had just turned seventeen, and I was hardly a kid. What in the world had gotten into him? He had always been an okay guy, but now he was acting decidedly strange. What was that comment about waiting for me to grow up? Whatever was going on with him, I decided that it was none of my concern. Yet I could still feel his eyes on me as I walked out of the kitchen to return to my friends.

I hadn't always been the only girl in our group. In elementary school there had been several other tomboys that played just as rough as the boys. That had changed in middle school as they suddenly developed crushes on boys and began to wear makeup and dress more girly.

It soon became apparent that they only wanted to be friends with me so they could be near my brother and his friends. By high school I was the only one who had no interest in dating. Connor and Jake, on the other hand, were two of the most popular boys at school.

Connor had the same ordinary brown eyes and brown hair as I did, but girls found him attractive for some reason. Sure, he was in good shape from playing basketball, but I didn't see why that made him any more appealing than any other guy. Jake, as I already mentioned had blue eyes. They were the kind of blue eyes that people noticed. Not that I paid any more attention to them than I did to anyone else's eyes.

It's just that girls at school always talked about his eyes. He also played basketball, but he must have done some kind of weight training too if the muscles in his arms were any indication. The only reason I had noticed his arms was because Kyle had said something about them. I was the only one who knew that Kyle was gay. His boyfriend went to another school, and Kyle had decided that his love life was nobody else's business. He only told me, his best friend since elementary school.

I was the only one of my friends who had never been on a date or had a crush on anyone. Kyle was waiting to see who would catch my interest, but nobody had so far. I loved being friends with guys, but I had no desire to date them. My parents had divorced when I was little, and I had watched my mom move from one failed relationship to another. My father was an alcoholic, and our visits with him had dwindled as his drinking got worse. Now we were down to talking on the phone from time to time.

Romantic relationships seemed like they weren't worth the trouble. They made it look so great in the movies, but real life didn't work that way. I had seen a lot of heartbreak around me, and it baffled me as to why people still kept trying to find true love.

"It's such a high when you're with that person," Kyle told me. "Just wait until your hormones kick in. You'll see." He had spotted Jake then. "Oh, hot damn! How can you have that delicious piece of eye candy practically living with you and not be drooling over him every day? Just look at his arms for one thing."

I surreptitiously glanced at Jake's arms. "He does look strong."

"Strong?" Kyle asked in disbelief. "He looks freaking hot! If only he wasn't straight…" He had trailed off dreamily.

I hoped that my hormones would never kick in if it meant I could avoid being obsessed with someone's body parts. I sure didn't want to drool over anyone. Kyle had said that it was a high, but I didn't need to be high that way. I got a rush when I was playing sports, and I had a warm and fuzzy feeling when I was with my family or friends. I was perfectly content with that.

After my friends went home that night when Jake had that strange conversation with me, I took a nice long shower. My room was right across the hall from the bathroom, so I always walked the few steps wrapped in a towel after my showers. It had never been a problem until that night. When I opened the bathroom door, Jake was leaning against the wall beside my room.

"Oh, sorry I took so long. It's all yours now." Even as I spoke, I wondered why I was apologizing. There was another bathroom downstairs.

He was studying me again, but his gaze was more intense than it had been in the kitchen earlier that evening. "You can't be walking around like that. You might not know that you're a girl, but any guy who sees you like this will never forget it. You could even give Kyle a hard on in that towel."

I looked at him in alarm. "What's that supposed to mean?"

He flashed a smile. "Don't worry. His secret's safe with me. I've seen you guys checking me out."

"I was not checking you out," I said in indignation.

"Whatever you need to tell yourself, Cam. What I'm worried about now is how clueless you are about walking around practically naked. Your buddies might get the wrong idea if they see you like this." He gestured toward my body. "You can't keep doing this."

Now I was getting really annoyed. Who did he think he was? "I can do whatever I want. This is my house. If you don't like it, you can leave."

His smile was different now. It seemed—dangerous. That didn't even make any sense. How could a smile be dangerous? He pushed off from the wall and stepped closer. "The problem is that I do like it. Remember what you guys were talking about before? About how a guy's body reacts to a hot girl? Do you see how much I like it?"

My eyes followed his hand down to where he indicated. I had seen him many times in just boxer shorts, but I hadn't ever noticed that reaction before. What an annoying thing to have to deal with, I thought. "Boy, I'm glad I'm not a guy."

His blue eyes traveled down the length of me one more time. "Me too, Cam. Me too." Then he walked away without even bothering to use the bathroom.

Chapter 2

"Wait, rewind." Kyle interrupted my story about Jake trying to order me around last night. "He told you that you're hot."

I shrugged. "I guess, but the point is that he's trying to tell me what to do in my own house."

"No, Cam, the point is that he thinks you're hot. How can you be so blasé about that?"

I popped another potato chip into my mouth. "I don't care what he thinks. I'll walk around here any way I damn well please."

Kyle's dirty mind was in direct contrast to his innocent-looking face. He looked positively angelic with his clear blue eyes and blond hair. "I second that. Next time accidentally drop your towel and bend over to pick it up."

"Kyle!" I protested with a laugh.

"Sorry, but I'll never have him so I have to live vicariously through you."

I became distracted by the porno movie we were watching on my computer. It had, of course, been Kyle's idea. We were stuffing our faces with potato chips and critiquing the performances. It had some kind of flimsy plot about a model who got into all kinds of erotic situations. To Kyle's delight, she had a ridiculous line that she kept using. It seemed to be her catchphrase, and we were keeping track of the number of times she said it.

"Oh, look at that. She's getting onto the bed with her high heels on," I commented. "You know they're going to snag on the sheets."

"I don't hear him complaining." He smiled at me. "That's probably the most girly thing I've ever heard you say."

"There's no reason to ruin perfectly good sheets. Hmm, do all girls shave their privates like that?" I crunched on more potato chips.

"How should I know?" Kyle asked.

"Oh, right." I said. "Well, it's bad enough having to shave our legs and underarms. Guys are lucky in that department."

"At least you can cover those parts up if you don't feel like shaving. We have to take care of our faces every day." He looked at me curiously. "Is any of this stuff turning you on?"

"Not really. It's basically all body parts. Real movies are sexier, because the characters are exciting." He had hit upon something that was troubling me. "I heard some girls at school talking about me. They think I'm gay."

"Those bitches," he said in mock outrage.

"The thing is, maybe I am. I mean, since I haven't been attracted to anyone. It's a possibility, right?" I spoke seriously, because I really wanted answers from him.

"You're attracted to Brad Pitt. Remember, you said he's hot after we watched World War Z. Plus, you've had crushes on other actors too. You've never said anything about having a crush on an actress."

I thought about it. "That's true, but maybe that's just social conditioning." Another idea occurred to me. "Or maybe I'm asexual."

"No, you're not." He immediately shot down that line of thinking. "You're just a late bloomer."

I poked him in the chest. "You just don't want to give up on me hooking up with Jake."

"Somebody's got to live the dream," he said solemnly.

"Pervert," I laughed. Then I batted my eyelashes at him. "Could you please go get me some more juice?"

"Oh. I, uh, finished the last of it." He cringed in preparation for my reaction.

"You drank all my juice?" I whined. "I thought you were my friend."

"Shush and watch the movie. I'm trying to corrupt you."

"Or distract me from what you did." I pretended to be put out.

He stuffed his mouth full of chips so he wouldn't have to answer. I rolled my eyes and turned back to the screen. The adult actors were getting pretty loud as they went at it.

Suddenly, we heard someone fling open my bedroom door and turned to see Jake storm in followed by Connor. Jake stopped short when he saw us.

"What happened?" I mumbled through a mouthful of chips.

"Want some?" Kyle's mouth was also full of chips as he held out the bag toward Jake and my brother.

"See? I told you she wasn't having sex," Connor said.

Jake walked over to see what we were watching. Kyle again offered him some chips, but he declined. Connor grabbed a handful and began munching on them.

"We're out of orange juice," I said.

"She had two glasses," Kyle hurried to tell Connor.

"He had three glasses." I stuck my tongue out at Kyle.

"What happened to your leg?" Jake asked me.

"Skateboarding accident. Kyle took care of it," I added grudgingly.

"Now you remember my good deeds. Shouldn't your hero get unlimited juice?"

"Hero?" I sniffed. "Ha! You bandaged a scrape."

"You should have heard her scream like a girl when I put disinfectant on it," Kyle confided to them.

I gave him the evil eye. "I did not!"

"I had to promise her porn to get her to hold still," he said, lying outrageously. "Of course, she wouldn't get hurt if she didn't try to keep up with Jason."

Jason was the best skateboarder in our group. He was cool about it, but my competitive nature sometimes made me try to top him. It wasn't the first time I'd gotten hurt trying to outdo him.

"You're lucky you didn't break your arm like last time," Connor chided me. It was Jake, however, that looked displeased with me.

"How do you want me?" The actress in the porno said her line again.

"Five!" Kyle and I cried out in unison and high-fived each other.

Jake looked from me to Kyle and shook his head. "At least you can't get hurt watching porno movies."

"Actually, one time," Kyle began some ridiculous tall tale before I kicked him with my good leg.

"I don't even wanna know," Connor said as he started to leave the room.

Jake glanced back at me one last time before he walked out, shutting the door behind him.

Kyle waited until he thought they were gone. "Did you see how he came charging in here when he thought you were having sex? And then he was all concerned about your leg. He's got it bad for you, Cam."

"Will you give it up already? I'm not hooking up with him just to make you happy." I clicked the porno movie off.

"Hey! I was watching that," he protested.

"No, you were just about to drive me to the store for more juice." I started shutting down my computer.

"You could have sex with Jake, but all you can think about is juice," Kyle grumbled.

Nothing changed until about a month later when Kyle and his boyfriend broke up. He took it very hard, and after days of moping and even missing a day of school, I decided that he needed me there and told him that I was sleeping over. Mom wouldn't even know that I was gone, because she was working until early morning and wouldn't be up until later in the day. I would be home by then. Connor and I always covered for each other, no questions asked. It was a Friday night, so I didn't have to get up for school.

Despite all my efforts, Kyle remained inconsolable. I had never seen him this way, and I realized that his feelings for his boyfriend ran much deeper than he had ever let on. Here was more proof to me that romantic relationships always ended in heartbreak. Only two hours into our evening, he got a phone call from his ex-boyfriend, who wanted to talk to him in person.

"I'm sorry, Cam," Kyle apologized, but he looked more hopeful than I had seen him since his breakup. "I can drop you off at home on the way to his house."

"I understand. Absolutely, go and talk to him. I hope you guys work it out." I gave him a hug.

"Thanks, Cam. You're the best." He hugged me back with all the unspoken affection that was between us.

Kyle drove me home and promised to call me tomorrow. I noted that Jake's car was parked in our driveway as well as Connor's. This surprised me since my brother had mentioned having a date tonight. Nobody was in the living room when I entered the house. I decided to take my shower first and then relax on the couch watching TV.

The first thing I noticed when I went upstairs was that the door to my room was closed, but I had left it open when I left. Then I heard the noises coming from behind the closed door. I marched over to it to give them a piece of my mind for using my computer to watch porno movies when Connor had his own computer. I threw open the door and stormed in only to stop dead in my tracks at the shocking sight before me.

At my entrance, the girl screeched while Jake reared up off of her and approached me. In those interminable first couple of minutes my eyes didn't know where to look. All I could see was flesh. Jake stood at least six feet tall, and there were no clothes to break up my view of his seemingly endless expanse of flesh.

I paid scant attention to the mortified girl and directed my anger squarely where it belonged. "You. In my room," I sputtered. "On my bed!"

His attitude only intensified my rage. He made no apology
or explanation, and he didn't even look embarrassed about being
caught having sex in my room. I tried to punch him, but he
anticipated my move with apparently lightning fast reflexes as he
grabbed my arm before my fist could connect with his face.
After all, he had been the one who taught me how to throw a
punch after I insisted on getting a punching bag. He had
watched my feeble attempts for a while before he stepped in to
show me the proper form. That had been two years ago.

Now he seemed to have completely forgotten about the
other girl in the room as his gaze locked with mine. His blue
eyes were darker than usual, and the way he was looking at me
made me understand what they meant by the word smoldering.

"Let go of me," I hissed.

As soon as he did, I spun around and sprinted out of the
room and down the hall to Connor's room. I ignored Jake
shouting my name as I flung open the door. Thankfully, the girl
was on top this time, and I was spared getting an eyeful of my
brother. I screamed in rage and slammed the door shut. Jake
was standing there when I turned around. He was still very
much naked. Even worse, he was laughing at me!
"Ow!" Jake cried after I kicked him in the shin.

"Get out of my house," I yelled.

He followed me back to my room. At least the girl had
enough sense to have made herself scarce. "How dare you?
This is my room, my bed."

"I thought you were sleeping over Kyle's house," he said as he put on his underwear.

"So that makes it okay? You're so gross. Were you even going to change the sheets?"

"These are my sheets. Yours are over there." He pointed to my desk. "You wouldn't have even known the difference."

"How thoughtful of you," I said sarcastically. Then I had a horrible thought. "How many times have you had sex on my bed?"

"Well, I was planning on at least three times tonight, but I didn't even get to finish once." He stripped his sheets off my bed and made a move to grab my sheets.

"Don't touch them!" I ran to the bathroom and came back with a can of Lysol. "You never answered my question," I said as I sprayed my mattress.

"Don't you think you're going overboard? How many people do you think have had sex in the same bed you sleep in when you go to a hotel?"

I suddenly had an entirely different view of past vacations out of town. "Stop trying to change the subject. How many times have you used my bed for sex?"

"I'll tell you what. I promise not to have sex in your bed anymore until it's with you." He pulled on his pants.

"If you think I'll ever let you touch me, you're crazy. If it were up to me, you'd never set foot in this house again. I'm warning you to stay the hell out of my way. Don't ever come near me or my room again. I hate you!" I was trembling with rage by the time I finished my rant against him.

He was infuriatingly calm as he put on his shirt. "We'll see about that, Cam. Goodnight."

I slammed the door after him. Connor, I knew, wouldn't dare face me until the next day. Jake was wrong if he thought this was just going to blow over. As far as I was concerned, he was now my enemy.

Chapter 3

I stood fuming in my room as I waited. Soon enough I heard someone go into the bathroom. My guess was Connor, and I waited until he left and everything was quiet again. Then I finally carried on with my plan to take a shower. As I began to take my clothes off in the bathroom, I spotted condoms in the wastebasket. The idiots hadn't even thought about concealing them from view. I threw a few tissues on top of them. Despite how mad I was, the instinct to cover for the guys was automatic. Unbidden, an old memory surfaced in my mind.

We were eight years old. Daddy had promised not to drink anymore. He had promised! Yet we were once again woken late at night by our parents yelling at each other. Connor crept into my room and cuddled with me as we listened to the familiar argument.

The next day was Saturday, and Connor's friend came over to play. Mom said to go to the playground, because Daddy was still sleeping. The boys wanted to play baseball, but I was just going to climb on the playground equipment. Connor said that he had to go to the bathroom, so Jake was waiting for him in our yard. I grabbed a baseball and marched toward the backyard.

Jake followed me. "Wanna play, Cam?"

"No," I answered tersely. Then I threw the baseball with all my might into my parents' bedroom window. It made a satisfyingly loud sound as it broke the glass.

"What the hell?" Daddy yelled. He appeared at the window a minute later and looked out at us. "You," he said to Jake, who was holding a baseball bat. "Haven't you been told not to play baseball in the yard?"

I opened my mouth to confess, but Jake beat me to it. "I'm sorry sir."

"You're damn right you'll be sorry. I'm gonna call your parents."

"What's all the commotion?" Mom asked as she came up behind Daddy.

"That damn kid broke my window," he said as he scowled at Jake.

"Watch your mouth in front of the children," Mom admonished. "It was an accident, Paul."

"How many times do we have to tell them not to play baseball in the yard? This is the third broken window. You're too soft with these damn kids, Dana."

"That wasn't Jake's fault. Connor broke the other two," Mom reminded him.

"And I paid to fix them, so now his parents can pay to fix this one."

"What's going on?" Connor asked when he found us in the backyard.

"Go on to the playground now kids," Mom said.

Despite Mom's objections, Daddy stubbornly followed through on his threat to call Jake's parents. They paid for the window and grounded him for disobeying our parents' rules. During the entire ordeal, Jake never said a word about what had really happened. I told Connor, and he said he knew that Jake was no tattletale.

I approached Jake on the playground since he wasn't allowed over our house while he was grounded. "I'm sorry I got you in trouble."

"It's okay." He smiled at me.

"Why'd you do that?" This had been bothering me since it happened. Why would anybody want to get in trouble on purpose?

He scuffed his shoe on the pavement as he looked down. "Just because."

Connor called to Jake to join the game he was playing. "Wanna play too, Cam?" Jake asked me.

"Okay." Now that I knew he wasn't mad at me, my guilt evaporated.

That was the only time we had ever talked about it. Jake never brought it up, not once, in all the intervening years. So he had done me a favor a long time ago, I thought. That didn't mean that I should forgive him for what he had done in my room behind my back. It was disgusting, and he hadn't even apologized.

I finished taking my shower and walked back to my room wrapped in a towel. This time I encountered no one in the hallway. After I put on my pajamas, I didn't even bother making up the bed with my sheets. There was no way I could sleep in it tonight. It was the couch for me, and I fell asleep while watching TV.

I woke up grouchy the next morning. "Don't talk to me," I snapped at Connor when I walked into the kitchen.

He gave me that puppy dog look with his brown eyes. "I'm sorry, Cam."

"You owe me a new mattress. How could you let him do that on my bed?" I kept my voice low so I wouldn't wake up Mom.

"He needed a place. You know his house is always full of people. Besides, he always uses his own sheets." As soon as the words were out of his mouth, Connor realized his mistake.

"Always?" I pounced like I hadn't already thought of that last night. "How many times has this happened?"

His eyes slid away from me. "A couple times."

I knew that he was lying, and I suddenly had no appetite for breakfast. "You jerk! How would you like it if my friends were having sex on your bed?"

"You don't understand what it's like, Cam. You're not a guy. You don't know what it's like when you're desperate for a place to be alone with your girl." This time he looked away in embarrassment. "Uh, last night."

I knew immediately what he was getting at. "Don't talk about that. I've blocked that from my mind permanently."

"Just knock next time." He sighed. "Not that it matters. I don't think Jen will ever come over again. It freaked her out pretty bad."

"Poor baby," I said with no sympathy at all. "That never would have happened if you hadn't let Jake use my room. Don't tell me he has no place to be alone, because he has his car."

"That's not exactly comfortable for guys our size," Connor said. He saw my expression and laughed. "Not size that way. I meant we're tall. I'm six foot, and Jake has two inches on me. Height wise," he clarified again.

Talking about this was making me extremely uncomfortable for the first time in my life. I had seen Jake's size in more ways than one. My guy friends were always talking about inappropriate things, and it had never fazed me. I had told the truth when I said that I had blocked out what I had seen when I walked in on Connor having sex. For some reason, I couldn't seem to do the same with my memory of Jake from last night. My mind kept returning to the way he had looked, and the way he had looked at me.

"I'll forgive you this time, but I'm warning you that I'll seek revenge if you ever let him set foot in my room again. I promise you that you won't like it." I narrowed my eyes at him.

He put up his hands in surrender. "Never again. He's on his own from now on."

I perked up. "Does that mean he's banned from this house?"

Connor looked affronted. "You know he's my best friend. Besides, he's your friend too."

"Not anymore," I said with finality.

"He makes one mistake, and he's out just like that? That's cold, Cam." He was obviously eager to put the shoe on the other foot, because he brought up something from last year. "What about when you took his car?"

"That's not the same." I thought back on that restless night shortly after I'd gotten my driver's license.

For some inexplicable reason, I had decided to go on a joyride. Jake's car was parked last in our driveway, so I'd swiped his keys and took off without telling anyone. I had driven around for a good hour while singing along to the radio before a flat tire had put an end to my fun. The only spare in the trunk was the little doughnut one that came with the car. Fortunately, I wasn't that far from home since I had already been on my way back. Sneaking back into the house, I almost had a heart attack when I ran into Jake in the dark.

"Where have you been?" He spoke quietly, so I couldn't tell if he was angry.

"For a ride. I got a flat and—"

"Shh." Jake brought my attention to footsteps upstairs. "Your mom got home early," he whispered. He led me downstairs into the basement.

"Crap! I left the door to my room open," I whispered. Now she might see that I wasn't there.

"I closed it for you," he whispered. "I got up to go to the bathroom and noticed you were gone. Then I heard her come home. She was in the shower when you got home."

We waited until we thought she might have gone to bed and cautiously made our way upstairs. I pulled him close and stood on tiptoe to whisper in his ear. "Thanks."

It was weird how loud his breathing sounded right then, I thought before I pulled away and eased my door open to slip into my room. He wasn't mad at me the next day about taking his car. I offered to pay for a new tire, but he wouldn't take my money.

"You used his car without permission, and he used your room," Connor said now.

"That's different. I didn't have sex in his car." I had to stop saying that word, because it made me think about last night.

"You could have," Connor reasoned. "And he never would have known the difference."

"I'm done with this conversation," I announced and stood up.

"Aren't you going to eat anything?" Connor gestured at the cereal box with his spoon.

"Not hungry." I walked upstairs to my room. My bare mattress was an unwelcome reminder of what had happened here last night, so I resolutely put my sheets back on my bed. Then I got dressed and brushed my teeth. That's when I realized that I had to get out of the house, so I went for a walk. When I came back, I was finally ready to eat something.

Later that day, Kyle called me to tell me that he had gotten back together with his boyfriend. It was great to hear him sounding like himself again. "Sorry I ditched you last night. I'll make it up to you with a fun sleepover now that I'm not such a drag. Is your mom working tonight?"

"No, she's off. Maybe we can do it next Friday night." My mom was big on all of us eating our meals together when she was home. It was our time to catch up with each other and have some family time.

"So, how was your night?" Kyle asked.

"I can't talk about it while Mom's home," I said, lowering my voice for that part.

Kyle's voice got louder in my ear. "What did I miss? Did something happen with Jake?"

"You could say that."

Apparently, my sour tone didn't register with him. "Are you freaking kidding me? It finally happened!"

"Do you want me to go deaf? Calm down. It's not what you think. And on that note, is that all guys think about?"

"You've been around us long enough to know that's all we think about," he answered at a normal volume. "It's never bothered you before, so what happened now?"

"I'll fill you in when I can. My mom's calling me for lunch. I'll talk to you later."

We had a nice day with Mom, just the three of us. After dinner, she suggested that we kick back on the couch and watch a movie. Connor said that Jake was coming over, and they were going to hang out in the basement. Mom said that she and I could watch a chick flick then. She occasionally insisted that I needed some girl time. Those were the only times that I watched romantic movies.

Mom got a phone call from her boyfriend and told me that she would be down soon to watch the movie with me. She went upstairs to her room to talk in private while I turned on the TV and idly flipped through different channels. I heard Jake arrive, and he stopped in the living room to talk to me while Connor went downstairs to the basement.

"What are you watching?"

I stared unseeing at the TV. "Nothing yet. Mom and I are going to watch a movie. You know, I thought you'd have enough decency not to show your face here for a while, but I should have known better."

"Something's different about you." He was silent for a moment. "Why won't you look at me, Cam?"

"Maybe because I hate you." I continued to ignore him, but I felt his eyes on me. I shifted on the couch, suddenly unable to find a comfortable position. "Aren't you supposed to be hanging out in the basement?" I asked in irritation.

He stepped in front of me and leaned down until I was forced to make eye contact with him. "You can't stop picturing me naked. Can you, Cam?"

Chapter 4

Damn him, but it was true. Last night kept replaying in my mind, but it was having the wrong effect. It was getting hard to tap into the fury I had felt then. What was wrong with me? I managed to glare at him. "Get out of my face."

He ignored that demand. "I would have walked around naked in front of you a long time ago if I knew that's what it would take for you to see me."

"What the hell are you talking about?" Now I was down to scowling at him. All I could see were his eyes. Had they always been that arresting shade of blue?

"You see me now the way I've seen you for a long time. You're finally aware of me as a guy the way I'm aware of you as a girl." He sat down beside me on the couch. "Will you go out with me, Cam?"

"What?" My brain seemed to be in some kind of fog. Nothing was making sense anymore.

"On a date, Cam. Will you go out on a date with me?" He was sitting close beside me but not touching as he waited for my answer.

"Date?" I asked stupidly. It was almost like he was speaking a foreign language with how slow I was at comprehension. His eyes seemed to be drawing me in, and I realized that I had been leaning unconsciously toward him.

I shot out of my seat like a rocket. "You expect me to go on a date with you after what you did?" I had belatedly remembered that there had also been a naked girl in my room last night. "Get it through your thick head that I don't want anything to do with you."

He stood up. "I only heard want and you." Then he smiled at me the way he had once before.

My brain was alert now and sending danger signals to me as he stepped closer. My entire body seemed to be alert the way it was when I was about to do something slightly dangerous while skateboarding. I was dismayed to realize that I felt the same kind of rush of anticipation.

"Sorry I took so long," Mom said as she hurried down the stairs.

Jake turned away from me to say hi to her. Then he said bye to me before heading down to the basement. Mom and I watched a romantic comedy, which didn't help take my mind off what had happened between me and Jake. I had never thought about guys asking me out on dates. I had never even thought about romance at all, except in relation to other people. It might sound strange that I didn't imagine myself in some kind of future relationship, but I was very much a person who lived in the moment.

Mom, of course, took this opportunity to engage in what she considered girls' night talk. She somehow picked up on something in my demeanor when she asked me if there was anything new with
my love life. "Has someone asked you out?"

"Yes," I admitted, deciding to get her opinion on this.

"A boy?" Mom asked uncertainly.

I smiled. So, she wasn't sure about my sexuality either. "Yes, a boy."

"What did you say?" She waited intently for my answer.

"I didn't know what to say. I was just so surprised." That last part was true. I had been surprised almost speechless.

"Is this one of your friends?" She must have some kind of mom radar to pick up on this stuff.

"Kind of." I had considered Jake a friend until last night.

"And now you're not sure how you feel about him," she said, astounding me again with her correct guess.

"Yeah. How do you know when you like someone? Romantically I mean."

"You've never had a crush on anyone?" Mom asked in surprise.

"No, and I've liked it that way. Some of the girls at school act crazy about boys half the time."

Mom smiled. "I've been lucky to be spared you being boy crazy. You're not fickle in your affections, so I suspect that if you think you like this boy romantically, then you probably do."

"But I don't want to like him," I protested. "I want things to stay the way they are."

"You can't stop life from changing, Cam," she said wistfully. "You and Connor are growing up. Sometimes I miss the days when you were little, but I can't stop time."

I gathered my courage to ask her the thing I had been wondering about for a long time. "Mom, why do you even bother with romantic relationships? They never seem to work out."

She looked at me with understanding. "That's what this is about, isn't it? Your lack of physical fear worries me, so I forget that you're emotionally sensitive. You're afraid of getting hurt that way. Yes, love is complicated and scary, but I think it's worth the risk. You can't let fear stop you from living your life."

"Whoa, nobody's talking about love," I said.

"Not yet," she added.

Kyle's take on the whole thing was more along the lines of what the hell are you waiting for? He had declared walking in on Jake having sex to be the second best thing that could happen to a person. The first, of course, would be to actually be the one having sex with him. "Who was the lucky girl? Does she go to school with us?"
"I'm not sure," I admitted. "She seemed kind of familiar, but I really didn't pay much attention to her."

He nodded his blond head. "Perfectly understandable. I wouldn't have been able to tear my eyes off Jake either."

"Yeah, about that. See, at the time I was mad. I was really mad," I explained. "That was the normal reaction, but now…" I bit my lip. "Now, when I think about it, it's not normal."

"In what way?" Kyle asked.

"Remember when we were watching the porno movie? I said it was just body parts. Well, that's the way this should be, but it's not." I looked at him to see if he could provide the answer to what had mystified me.

"It's alive!" Kyle said in a Doctor Frankenstein voice.

"This isn't funny," I said in consternation. "I don't know why—"

"You don't know why you're turned on by a hot guy who's completely into you? I love you, Cam, but only you could be that clueless about your hormones. Remember when I said that you're a late bloomer? Well, baby you're blooming."

"I'm turned on?"

"Oh my God!" Kyle pretended to slam his head into the steering wheel. "Are you really in that much denial?"

Since I had refused to talk about what had happened over the weekend inside the school where somebody might overhear, we were sitting in Kyle's car during lunch so he could hear all the details. I had been relieved that Jake hadn't come over on Sunday, because I had no idea how to deal with him.

"We need to get back," I said. "Lunch is almost over."

"We should go shopping after school. You need to dress like a girl for your first date with Jake."

I had been just about to open the car door, but I turned back to look at him. "I already told you that I'm not going out with him."

Kyle looked genuinely perplexed. "Why not? You already know that you're attracted to him."

"No, that's just your theory. Besides, I caught him having sex with another girl in my room."

He rolled his eyes at me. "You're still hung up on that? That was—"

"Three days ago," I supplied. "He just had sex with another girl three days ago, so why is he asking me out?"

"Because obviously that's all it was with her. Just sex," he said.

"Then how do I know that's not all he wants from me?"

"That would be more than enough for me," Kyle quipped. He held up his hand to stop my retort. "Seriously, I think he really likes you. Look how worried he was that you might be having sex with someone else. If you want to test him, you could go out with someone else and see how jealous he gets."

"You're no help at all with your schemes, and we have to go before we're late."

Despite what I had said, Kyle had given me a lot to think about. How did I feel about Jake? Was I attracted to him, and if I was, was that all there was between us? My complete lack of romantic experience was a hindrance to me in this case. I had a crazy idea, but I decided to go with it. Nobody was there when I got home from soccer practice on Tuesday, so I called Kyle and asked if he could come over.

"Sure," he said. "What's going on?"

"I need to ask you a favor, but I'll tell you when you get here. Give me about half an hour to take a shower first."

Kyle knew where we kept the spare key, so I wasn't worried about him standing outside waiting for me to open the door. It took me awhile to get ready, because I washed and blow dried my long hair. It was still a little damp, because I was in a hurry to talk to Kyle, so I left it down. He was playing a video game in the living room when I went downstairs. I grabbed the remote and turned off the TV.

"Hey! I was winning," he protested.

"Later." I listened for a moment. "Are we alone?"

Kyle rubbed his hands together. "Ooh, secrets."

"Are we alone?" I asked again.

"Yeah, what's the big mystery? Did something else happen with Jake? Are you ready to have sex with him?"

I rolled my eyes. "Come back from perverted land. It's nothing to do with him. It's about me. I want you to teach me how to kiss."

Kyle laughed and then saw that I was serious. "I'm flattered, but why don't you ask Adam or Jason or any of the other guys? I'm pretty sure they're straight."

"That's exactly why I'm asking you," I explained. "I don't want things to be weird with them."

"Cam, it's sweet that you want to impress Jake, but I don't think it's necessary."

"I told you that this has nothing to do with him. I'm just trying to figure some stuff out for myself. Now, are you going to help me or not?" I demanded.

"Come here." He patted the seat beside him on the couch.

"Maybe we should go to my room in case somebody comes home."

Kyle feigned a hurt look. "Ashamed to be seen kissing me?"

Even though he was joking, there was an underlying challenge in his words. I had never been one to back down from a challenge, so I planted myself next to him. I wasn't sure what to do, but Kyle had no problem taking the lead. He tilted my chin and leaned in to kiss me. What was surprising to me was how enjoyable kissing was. His lips were soft against mine and caused a pleasant tingling sensation. I found myself getting into it until I abruptly ended the kiss.

I stared at him incredulously. "Did you just feel me up?"

"I just wanted to give you an authentic experience. How was it?"

"I could have skipped the groping, but the kissing was really good," I said.

"Don't sound so surprised. You're not the first girl I've ever kissed. In fact, my first sexual experience was with a girl."

I looked closely at him for a sign that this was another one of his made up stories, but he seemed sincere. "You never told me that. I thought you weren't attracted to girls."

"I'm not, but my body responded to her stimulation."

Now I was really confused. "How is that possible?"

"She went down on me," he explained. "When you close your eyes, it all feels the same." The mischievous glint that entered his eyes told me that the next thing he said would be a joke. "So, if you ever want me to teach you how to—"

Jake exploded out of the kitchen and into the living room. "You're not teaching her another damn
thing you sneaky little pervert!"

I jumped up out of my seat. "Where do you get off calling him a pervert? You had sex in my room!"

"And it wasn't even with her," Kyle added.

"Shut up, Kyle," I yelled. I turned back to Jake. "Don't you ever go home? Why are you always here?"

"Why is *he* always here?" Jake countered.

"You're just jealous that I got further with her than you did," Kyle said.

I threw myself in front of Kyle as Jake moved to attack him. "Leave him alone."

"Well, my work here is done," Kyle announced. "See you at school, Cam."

"I'll walk you out," I said as Jake backed off.

I noticed that Kyle had parked behind Jake in our driveway. "Wait a minute. You knew that he was here!"

He winked at me. "Now you have proof of his jealousy."

"So, it was all for show? Was any of that stuff you said even true?" I asked.

"All of it." His expression was very serious now. "I was confused for a long time after what happened with her. What I told you about how it can be just sex is true. When you find that special person, though, there's a spark there that you don't have with just anyone."

I smiled at him. "I'm glad you found your special person. Thanks for helping me out."

"Anything for you, Cam." Because he couldn't stay serious for too long, he had to add something outrageous. "I just hope I haven't ruined you for other men. They won't be able to compare with my legendary skills."

"Guess I'll have to become a nun then," I said with a smile.

"Not again!"

I laughed. "As much as I hate to see you leave, I have to do my homework."

"You can always do Jake instead." He ducked into the car before I could hit him. "I'm going, I'm going."

He honked the horn and waved before he drove away. I took a deep breath and walked back into the house. Jake was waiting for me right by the front door. "Did you figure it out?"

His question threw me. "Figure what out?"

"You said that you wanted him to teach you how to kiss so you could figure something out for yourself," Jake said.

So he had heard the whole thing. "I'm still working on it."

He stepped closer, and I immediately stepped back. "Can I help?"

"Yes," I said. "You can leave me alone."
"I love when you wear your hair down like that. You've got such beautiful hair." He took another step closer.

I took another step back and came up against the door. "Where's Connor?"

"At his girlfriend's house. Her parents are out of town all week." He reached out to touch my hair. "It's so thick and beautiful."

"But his car is here." It was bizarre to be carrying on a conversation with him while he touched my hair lovingly.

"She picked him up so your mom wouldn't know he wasn't home. I want to kiss you, Cam." His voice sounded different now.

My heart had started beating faster. "You mean he'll be gone all night? Why are you here when he's not?"

"I volunteered to stay here and make sure that you're safe. May I kiss you, Cam?"

I closed my eyes. "Yes."

His hand moved to the back of my head and pulled slightly forward. With my eyes closed, I didn't see him lean down, but I felt his warm breath before his lips touched mine. My lips were tingling in anticipation even before we made contact, but the kiss was nothing short of electric. Kyle had said that Jake turned me on, and now I couldn't deny it any longer. I molded my body to his as I was consumed with the passion of our kiss. Jake responded by deepening the kiss until we were breathless.

I leaned back against the door and breathed heavily until I could speak. "I figured it out now."

Chapter 5

"What did you figure out?" Jake asked.

"It's sex." I looked at him and wondered how I had failed to notice how sexy he was before now.

Even his smile was sexy. "What did you figure out about sex?"

"It's what's between us," I said. "Once we get that out of the way, we can go back to normal."

His smile disappeared. "What do you mean get it out of the way?"

"You were right when you said that I can't stop thinking about you naked," I admitted. "I need to have sex with you to get it out of my system, and then I'll stop thinking about you that way."

Jake didn't seem too happy with my plan. "What do you know about sex? You only just had your first kiss today."

"I know the basics of what to do. Besides, you know all about it, and you said that you wanted to have sex with me," I reminded him.

The passion had faded from his eyes, and he now looked upset with me. "I said that I wanted to go out with you."

"Isn't that the whole point of dating? You get to know each other so you can have sex. My friends are always talking about how many dates they have to go on before they can have sex. We already know each other, so we can skip right to the sex. Anyway, we have the house to ourselves this week, so this is the perfect time to get it done."

Now his anger flared. "You wouldn't have such a screwed up idea of dating if you were friends with girls. Guys don't tell their friends everything, Cam."

"Like what?" I asked in bewilderment. I had thought that he'd be enthusiastic about having sex with me. He had made it clear that he was attracted to me.

Instead of answering me, he asked his own questions. "Why can't we have a normal relationship? If you like me enough to have sex with me, then what's wrong with being my girlfriend?"

"I don't want that. I just want to go back to the way things were before. I don't understand what the problem is. It's not like you haven't done this before. Obviously, that girl wasn't your girlfriend or you wouldn't be asking me out. It was just sex, right?"

"And that's all you want from me, Cam? Just sex?" He regarded me with a sullen expression.

"I want to put this whole thing behind us." I was disappointed that the mood between us had deteriorated so quickly.

"Do you really think that it'll be that easy to go back to just being friends?" He let out an exasperated breath. "You don't even know what you're talking about. You have no experience with this."

"I don't understand you, Jake. You said that you weren't going to have sex in my room until it was with me, and now you don't want to."

"I do want to, but not like this." He looked just as disappointed as I felt. "Go do your homework or something."

I couldn't believe it. I had just been dismissed in my own house. My shoulder knocked into his arm as I stormed past him. He couldn't make up his damn mind about what he wanted. My solution was simple, and it would have solved the problem. In my distress, I wandered into my parents' old bedroom. Here was more proof that romance ended in misery. Mom had turned this room into an office after the divorce, and she had taken a bedroom upstairs. She apparently couldn't bear to sleep in this room alone after sharing it with Dad.

I did have to get my homework done, so I went up to my room to start on it. Jake appeared in my doorway about an hour later and told me that dinner was ready. He was often the one who cooked meals when he was over during the week. Mom thought it was great, because she always had leftovers for lunch the next day.

I remember being surprised as a child that he already knew how to cook, but he had told me that he helped his mom prepare the meals since they had a large family. Connor seemed to always sleep in longer on the weekends than Jake and I, and I had many memories of the two of us making breakfast together.

He actually taught me more about cooking than my mom had. We had an easy companionship back then, but now we ate our spaghetti in silence. I loaded the dishwasher while Jake went to do his homework.

I didn't see him after my shower when I defiantly walked out into the hallway wrapped in my towel. Later on, I heard the shower running when I left my room to use the bathroom, so I went downstairs. We both had cereal for breakfast in the morning and parted ways in the driveway. I drove Connor's car to school so Mom wouldn't know that he hadn't been home. She had bought the car for us to share, but he seemed to drive it more than I did since he had a girlfriend. I usually rode with him to school, but often got a ride from one of my friends depending on what we did after school.

Kyle and I ate lunch in his car again while I told him about my evening with Jake. He was thrilled at first when I told him about Jake kissing me. Then I managed to shock him for the first time in my life when I told him about wanting to have sex with Jake.

He was giving me an odd look by the end of my story. "You hurt his feelings, Cam."

I hadn't expected that response. "By offering to have sex with him?"

"By telling him that you wanted to have a one-night stand and move on. The fact that he turned down no strings attached sex says that he likes you a lot," Kyle said.

"He wants me to be his girlfriend, but I can't deal with that."

"Why not?" Kyle asked.

"Look at how miserable you were when Scott broke up with you. I don't want anyone to have that kind of power over me." I had never told this to anyone before.

"The reason he broke up with me was because I was keeping him a secret. You're the only one who knew about him, but all his friends knew about me. We even went to a few dances at his school. He felt like he wasn't important to me. Guys don't talk about it, but we have feelings too. I hate to break it to you, Cam, but avoiding relationships isn't going to make you immune to love."

I wasn't following him on that one. "What do you mean? I need to be part of a couple to be in love."

Kyle shook his head. "It doesn't always work that way. Just because you're not dating Jake doesn't mean you don't have feelings for him. He has feelings for you even though you're not his girlfriend."

"I don't have any feelings for him," I said confidently. "It's just physical attraction."

"You didn't even know you were attracted to him, so who knows what other feelings you have for him? Why don't you go out with him and see what happens?" Kyle suggested.

I was determined to do things my way. My plan now was to ignore all my thoughts about Jake until they went away. Now that he wasn't trying to get my attention, it would be easy to avoid him.

Chapter 6

Kyle and I had to postpone our sleepover again, because I had to come home to cover for Connor. It was his last night sleeping over his girlfriend's house, and I couldn't expect Jake to stay at our house alone. Kyle said that he would be fine as long as I was at the dance. This was his first time bringing a date, and our friends were curious about who it was. Kyle had decided not to say anything and just let them see for themselves. They didn't know that he was coming out of the closet tonight. I hadn't been to a school dance since elementary school, and the only reason I was going now was to support Kyle.

"Are you nervous?" I asked him the day before the dance.

"A little," he admitted. "But I've decided that I'd rather lose all my other friends than lose Scott again."

I couldn't believe that they would drop him just like that. Most of us had been friends since elementary school, so I thought that our bond was too strong to be broken. Sure, they would be surprised, but I was confident that they would accept his sexual orientation after the shock wore off.

Kyle was dismayed at what I had chosen to wear to the dance. "Why don't you come out too, Cam? I don't know what would shock them more, me being gay or you being a girl."

"Ha! Ha! Very funny." I looked down at the black boy's track pants and black t-shirt I was modeling for Kyle. "Who cares what I wear? I'm only going because of you."

45

"No wonder Jake doesn't want to have sex with you," Kyle said.

I rolled my eyes. Jake was actually driving me to the dance and had assured me that this wasn't a date. "It's stupid to drive separately when we're going to the same place."

"Won't your date mind?" Why had I asked him that? I sounded like one of those pathetic girls fishing for information.

"I don't have a date," he said with a pointed look at me. "Kyle told me about tonight, and I told him I'd be there."

"He did? I thought you didn't like him." The last exchange I'd seen between them hadn't been very friendly.

"He'd just offered to teach you how to give him a blow job, so I wasn't thinking straight. I realized after that he was just kidding."

I smiled. "He's joking about eighty percent of the time, but tonight is serious. That's very nice of you to show moral support."

"Yeah, well I guess we better get ready." He went off into Connor's room and closed the door.

After much pleading from Kyle, I had agreed to wear my hair down for the dance. "It'll take some of the attention off me," he'd joked.

I tried to remember how long it had been since my friends had seen it down. I had it up in a ponytail ninety percent of the time so it wouldn't be in my way for all the physical activities I engaged in. I wasn't really sure why I didn't just cut my hair short. It sure did make me look more girly, even without any makeup, which I didn't own and wouldn't have known how to apply anyway. For some inexplicable reason, I went into Mom's room and sprayed on some of her perfume. It didn't take me any longer to get ready than Jake. Fortunately, this was a casual dance. Jake, however, had opted to wear dress pants and a dark blue short-sleeved dress shirt.

He grinned when he saw me. "I like it!"

Then he impulsively pulled me to stand in front of the hallway mirror beside him. As I gazed at our reflections, I noticed how much lighter his brown hair was than mine. Jake looked so good that I couldn't understand what he saw in me. Okay, my hair looked pretty enough to be used in one of those commercials on TV, but that was arguably my best feature. Jake was gorgeous from head to toe. I knew exactly what kind of body was under those clothes. Oh, not again! I had to stop thinking about that.

"What's wrong, Cam?" He was watching my reflection in the mirror.

"I want you to kiss me again," I blurted without thinking.

In an instant, he had spun around and brought his lips crashing down on mine. My passion ignited instantaneously too, and I couldn't get close enough to him fast enough. I grabbed onto his shoulders and swung my legs up around his waist so I could be level with his face and get deeper into his kiss. He leaned me up against the wall as his tongue tangled with mine. My hands were in his hair as his hands gripped my hips while he pressed himself into me. I heard myself moan for the first time ever. It felt so good that I didn't want it to stop.

Jake groaned and pulled his mouth away from mine. The look in his blue eyes sent a thrill through me. All I could do was cling to his shoulders and take shallow breaths. He extricated himself from me and set me down while he backed up and leaned against the wall across from me. He closed his eyes as he took his own shallow breaths, but I couldn't look away from him as I sagged against the wall behind me.

"Why'd you stop?" I knew that he had been enjoying it just as much as I had.

His eyes were still a darker shade of blue than usual as they snapped open to look at me. "The dance." He cleared his throat. "Let's go."

I followed him downstairs and out to his car. My mind wasn't on the dance but on what would happen after we got back to the empty house. Would we have sex? There had been a charged atmosphere between us all week. My plan to ignore him hadn't worked out too well. Instead of dissipating, my attraction to him seemed to be increasing with each passing day.

The looks he sent my way weren't helping either. We had been doing our homework at the
kitchen table after dinner one evening. I had been concentrating on figuring out a math problem when I happened to glance across at Jake. His eyes were on my mouth as I chewed on my nail. My hand slowly dropped to the table as Jake met my gaze. The way he was looking at me made me think that he was going to kiss me, but he gathered his books and left the kitchen.

The following night, Jake happened to walk out of Connor's room as I stepped out of the bathroom in my towel. Our eyes met across the hallway, and then his gaze slowly traveled down my body. His eyes seemed to be burning a trail along all my nerve endings as they reached my feet and started back up my body. By the time his gaze returned to my face, my heart was racing wildly.

I clutched at my towel as I took the steps to my room. Jake took a few steps toward me, and I stopped at the entrance to my room and waited to see if he would follow me to my bed. He must have seen the question in my eyes, because he stopped and shook his head. It took me a long time to fall asleep that night.

Now that he had kissed me again, I was hoping that he had changed his mind about having sex with me so that we could finally put an end to the attraction between us. We were among the first people to get to the dance, but Kyle and Scott were already there.

Kyle didn't want to make an entrance but just casually introduce Scott as his date when the rest of the guys arrived with their dates. They were all polite about meeting Scott, but I could tell that they were shocked. Their dates seemed to take it in stride, but didn't seem to know what to make of me. A few of my friends did double takes when they saw me. They shot curious glances at me and Jake, who remained by my side the whole time.

Everything went well until Chad met Scott. He stared at Kyle. "You're queer?"

My hackles rose. "He's gay."

Chad sneered at me. "Figures you'd stick up for him. You're probably a lesbian."

I was pissed at his attitude, but I kept my voice even. "So what if I am? How does that change our friendship?"

"I'm not gonna be friends with a bunch of queers." He turned to Kyle. "You shouldn't even be allowed in the boys' bathroom, you freak."

"Don't worry, Chad. You're not my type," Kyle said.

"How can you act like this?" I demanded. "You've been friends with us for two years." Chad was the newest member of our group.

He turned his attention to me as his embarrassed date looked on. "It's a shame, Cam. You're actually kind of pretty. Too bad Kyle's the one who likes dick."

So, yeah, I punched him in the nose. He hadn't had a chance to recover from that before Jake hit him in the jaw and knocked him on his ass. Then he pulled me into one hell of a kiss. "Not that it's really any of your business, Chad, but she's not a lesbian. That still doesn't mean that you would ever have a chance with her."

The three of us got kicked out of the dance for fighting on school property. Chad protested that he hadn't done anything, but the teachers who were chaperoning the dance said that the principal would sort that all out on Monday. I didn't care that I had gotten in trouble.

I had lost a friend tonight, but I decided that he hadn't been a real friend in the first place. He had shown an ugly side that I had never seen before. Jake, however, had come through for me and Kyle, even though he had kissed me in front of everyone. I would ponder the significance of that later. Right now, my mind was on what would happen once we got back to my house.

Chapter 7

I launched myself at Jake as soon as he shut the front door. Even in his surprise, his reflexes were perfect as he caught me and supported my weight with his hands under my rear while I wrapped my legs around him. He made some kind of startled sound before I pressed my lips to his. Then we were kissing as passionately as we had before the dance. We somehow made it over to the couch, and he leaned over and deposited me onto it.

Then he sat down beside me. "We have to talk."

I didn't want to stop to talk, so I distracted him by straddling his lap. He managed to say my name once before I kissed him again. I had initiated the kiss, but Jake quickly became the aggressor as he tangled his hand in my hair and hungrily explored my mouth with his own.

When he stopped to take in air, I yanked my shirt up over my head. I wanted to keep the momentum going so he wouldn't have time to change his mind. The fact that I was wearing a sports bra instead of some lacy Victoria's Secret number didn't stop Jake's eyes from roaming there. I always bought sports bras that flattened my chest as much as possible, because I didn't want to feel any bouncing while I was running around. Now the material felt constricting, and I moved to take it off.

"Don't." Jake had grabbed my hands, and his blue eyes were burning into mine. He let go of my hands and grasped me by the waist to lift me off his lap and set me back on the couch beside him. He leaned back and closed his eyes.

I slouched back in disappointment and wondered if lingerie would have enticed him into giving me what I wanted. I had literally thrown myself at him, and he had still rejected me. There was no doubt that he wanted me, because I could still see the proof of his arousal against his pants. Why was he being so stubborn about this?

"Do you like me, Cam?"

My eyes flitted back up to his face as I ran my hand suggestively up his thigh. "I thought that was obvious."

His own hand shot out to stop the progression of my hand. "I know you like my body, but do you like me?"

I considered the question. "I know I said that I hated you when I got mad, but I don't. You're still a good friend to me and Connor. Thanks for keeping me company this week. That was sweet of you, even though I can take care of myself."

"This week was…difficult. You don't know how many times I had to stop myself from waking you up and…" There was a look in his eyes that sent a delicious shiver through me.

"Why did you stop yourself?" I asked softly, trying not to disturb the mood.
He took a moment to compose himself. "I wanted to wait until we were going out awhile before I told you how I feel." When he caught my gaze again, his eyes were just as intense, but in a different way. "I've always liked you, Cam. Always."

"I liked you too," I said, unsure of where he was going with this.

"You don't understand." He sounded frustrated with me.

"You're right. I don't understand. I want you, and you want me. What's the problem?"

"I want more than that with you, Cam." He took my hand as he spoke. "Kyle told me that you're afraid to be in a relationship, but you have nothing to be afraid of with me. My feelings for you haven't changed in all this time." A hint of his sexy smile made an appearance. "Well, except in a certain way. I never thought about you naked when we were kids."

I instinctively pressed my advantage. "You can do more than just think about me naked," I offered.

He stunned me by how well he could read me. "This is not a game, Cam. I'm not your opponent."

I dropped my attempt to seduce him and turned to anger instead. "Kyle had no right to tell you my business."

"Stop avoiding the issue, Cam. This is not about Kyle. It's about me and you. I want to know how you feel about me. We can work through everything else if I know that you like me as much as I like you."
Something like panic overwhelmed me, and I tore my hand from his and stood up in a sudden need to put distance between us. "What do you want me to say?"

He regarded me in silence as the fire faded from his eyes. "You don't have to say it, Cam. I thought things would be different when I saw that you were attracted to me. I guess I was just fooling myself."

I couldn't stand to see his bleak expression. "Jake—"

"No, it's okay. You can't help how you feel." His eyes took on a look I didn't like as they swept over my body. The appraisal was cold this time. "I'll take you up on your offer someday, Cam. I just need some time to get over you first."

He stood up and went upstairs without saying anything else. Not knowing why I was so upset, I stood there fighting back tears until I got myself under control. Then I went upstairs to get ready for bed. Sleep wouldn't come, and I tossed and turned until I heard Mom come upstairs and start running the water in the bathroom.

I waited for a while after everything was quiet and I was sure she had gone to bed. Then I quietly slipped out of my room and down the hall to ease open the door to Connor's room. The moonlight streaming in through the window revealed an empty bed. I went downstairs to look outside and saw that Jake's car was already gone.

Chapter 8

Jake didn't make an appearance at our house the rest of the weekend. Connor was in a good mood Saturday morning when he returned from his girlfriend's house. He went to crash in his room, so he ended up sleeping in just like any other weekend. I was glad that Mom had a date that evening, because it was difficult enough trying to hide my bad mood during lunch and dinner.

She was pleasantly surprised to hear that I had attended the school dance. "Was it a date?"

"No," I snapped. She glanced at me sharply, so I told her about getting kicked out and about the meeting with the principal that awaited me on Monday.

"I don't condone violence, but I can see how you lost your temper. That must have been awful for Kyle," Mom said.

Connor was delighted. "Too bad I missed that. I'm surprised Jake didn't tell me about it."

"Did you talk to him today?" I asked casually. Connor obviously hadn't heard about what else had happened at the dance, or he would have said something about it to me.

"Yeah, he said he had family stuff to do tonight." Connor shrugged.

"I'm sure they missed him all week," Mom said. "It was a good week for leftovers here," she sighed. "That boy can cook.

He's going to make a great husband for some lucky girl." She smiled at me. "I know my cooking can't compare to Jake's, but it's not that bad. You could at least take a few bites."

Damn! She had noticed. "I'm just not hungry."

"How are you not hungry? You hardly touched your food at lunch."

Did she have to see everything? "I had a big breakfast," I lied.

I thought that was the end of it until she asked me to keep her company while she got ready for her date. "So, you really like this guy, huh?"

I was startled by her question. "What?"

"I know all the signs. You can't eat. You can't sleep." She answered my stunned expression. "Yeah, Cam, I can see how exhausted you look today."

"I was just upset about how Chad treated Kyle."

She wasn't buying it. "You don't have to tell me if you don't want to. I just want you to know that I'm here if you want to talk."

There was no way that I could tell my mom that Jake was upset with me because I wanted to have sex with him and nothing else. "Okay. Thanks, Mom."

I had called Kyle earlier in the day to find out how he was doing after last night. He was obviously fine, because he immediately started questioning me about my date with Jake. "It wasn't a date," I said.

"Of course it was," he said breezily. "Do you really think I needed Jake there for moral support? I thought you would see right through that. Too bad you didn't get to dance with him before you got kicked out. It was sooo romantic when he kissed you though. Everyone was talking about it."

"That's great," I said sarcastically.

Kyle was uncharacteristically quiet for a moment. "What happened now?"

"I'll tell you later."

"How could you screw things up after that great exit?" Kyle demanded.

"Me?" I huffed. "Why do you immediately assume it was me?"

"Because Jake likes you enough to ask me for advice about you." Kyle sighed. "Scott and I are going on a date tonight."

"Then it'll have to wait until Monday. Mom's home all day tomorrow."

Madison approached me on Monday before I had a chance to talk to Kyle. We had gym class together, but she had never said two words to me before. She was one of the popular, pretty girls that definitely dressed like a girl.

She pulled me off to the side after the teacher told us to do our warm up exercises, and that he would be right back. "Look, Cameron. I just wanted to say I'm sorry. I feel terrible about what happened, and I swear that I didn't know about you and Jake when he took me to your house."

Something clicked as I looked at her. "That was you?"

Her embarrassment turned to surprise. "I thought you saw me."

"I did, but I didn't recognize you." The truth was that she had barely registered with me, but there was no need to tell her that.

"Oh, well, I hope you can forgive me. I had no idea that Jake was your boyfriend."

"He's not my boyfriend," I said.

Her confusion was evident on her face. "But he kissed you at the dance."

I should have expected this after Kyle told me that people were talking about it. "That doesn't mean that he's my boyfriend."

"So, it's just a casual thing?" Madison asked.

"Yeah. It doesn't mean anything." I was glad to set her straight, and I hoped that the talk about Jake being my boyfriend would quickly die down.

"Hmm," she said thoughtfully. "You even think like a guy. I wish I could be like that. Guys are so afraid of commitment, so it would be much easier if I didn't get attached."

Thankfully, the teacher returned then, because I was already getting bored with this conversation. Gym was my favorite class, and I especially felt ready to lose myself in physical activity today. I had gone for a long run yesterday, and it had helped me sleep better than the previous night. The only problem was that I'd had a damn sex dream about Jake. This had never happened to me before, and I hoped that I wouldn't be dreaming about him on a regular basis.

I got detention for two weeks for punching Chad at the dance. We all got called in separately to see the principal, so I didn't know what happened to Jake and Chad. When I saw Jake in detention after school, he didn't say a word to me.

It bothered me more than I had expected it to. We had never been best friends, but we had always been friendly. Later on that evening I would hear from Connor that Jake also got two weeks of detention, while Chad got off with a warning. Connor was more interested in what happened between me and Jake at the dance, but I told him it was none of his business. He complained that Jake had also refused to talk about it.

Kyle sat in complete silence after I told him about Friday night. I looked out the windshield of his car and waited for him to say something. His tone held awe when he finally spoke. "He's completely in love with you."

My head whipped around toward him. "Where are you getting that from?"

"My God, Cam! How can you not see it?"

He never said that," I insisted.

"Read between the lines. Of course he couldn't say those actual words. You weren't exactly receptive to his feelings."

I remembered Jake's bleak expression, and how he'd said that he needed time to get over me. I still didn't want to believe that he had been talking about love. "He'll get over it."

"Eventually," Kyle agreed. "He won't wait around for you forever, so you better figure out how you feel about him."

I knew that Kyle was upset about this situation, because he didn't crack any jokes. He told me that he thought I was making a big mistake in not giving Jake a chance. "It's not so easy to find what you have with him. Go out with some other guys and you'll see what I mean."

The funny thing was that guys started asking me out the very next day. It began with Dylan, the most notorious player in our school. "Hi, Cameron. How's it going?"

I fought the urge to look behind me to make sure that he was really talking to me. "Good."

"That's good." He watched me with his dark eyes as a seductive half-smile played over his lips. Dylan had been described as sex on legs, and now I could see why. Everything he did oozed sex appeal, from the way he leaned against the locker next to me to the way he spoke in that low, intimate voice. "Will you come to Kayla's party with me, Cameron?"

"Why?" I asked in bewilderment.

"Just to hang out. It'll be fun. You like fun, don't you?" Someone passed by and called a greeting to him. He raised his hand in acknowledgement but never took his eyes off me.

How could I respond to that? "Sure, I like fun, but—"

"Good." The bell rang and he waited for it to stop. "I'll get your number in English. See you later, Cameron." He took off down the hall before I could protest.

Did I want to go to a party with him? The only parties I had ever attended were birthday parties for family and friends. This would be a completely different kind of party. Maybe it would be fun to try something different for a change. At least I didn't have to worry about Dylan wanting a relationship. I hardly knew him, so I certainly wasn't going to sleep with him. I was feeling restless and out of sorts since this whole thing with Jake. Maybe a party was just the distraction that I needed.

I gave Dylan my number in English class, and he gave me his and said he'd call me later. Another guy asked me out later that day, but I turned him down. I couldn't fathom why guys were suddenly interested in me.

Connor was the first one to give me a clue about it. "Did you and Jake have sex?"

I finished putting on my seatbelt and looked at him. "No."

"Are you sure?" Connor asked.

"I think I would know for sure. Are you going to drive, or should I?"

He turned on the ignition and pulled into the line of cars waiting to exit the school parking lot. "It's just that I heard a lot of people talking about it today."

"It's probably because of what happened at the dance," I said.

"I guess. Anyway, about that…"

"I'm not talking about that." I turned to stare out the window.

"Neither is Jake. What the hell is going on with you guys? He doesn't want to come over anymore."

"I'm sorry, Connor. I just don't want to get into it. Just give it some time, and things will go back to normal."

When Dylan called me later that evening, I was brusque with him. He didn't seem to take offence at my attitude, and he was as smooth as ever while he told me the details of the party. Then he tried to continue the conversation, but I cut him off. "Look, I'll go with you to the party, but you don't really need to talk to me until then."

Apparently, even his laugh was sexy. "I like a girl who knows what she wants. Okay, Cameron. Goodnight then."

"Goodnight, Dylan."

I was walking toward the cafeteria with Kyle the next day when Jake suddenly grabbed my arm and dragged me with him down the hall. I looked back at Kyle, who was watching us with amusement. There would be no help from him. I looked at Jake and saw that he was furious. Well, I was mad too. "What are you doing?"

He pushed open the door and pulled me outside with him. "My car," he spat at me.

"Let go of me. What about your car?"

He loosened his grip on my arm but didn't let go as he propelled me toward the parking lot. When we got to his car, I couldn't see anything wrong with it. He yanked open the passenger door for me as he finally let go of my arm. I glared at him, but I got into the car. "You don't even have lunch this period," I said after he got into the driver's side and shut the door. "Are you skipping class? You already have detention."

"Did you tell everyone that we had sex?" The words were spoken in a harsh tone that he had never used with me before.

I couldn't believe that he would accuse me of such a thing. "No. Why would I?"

"Because that's what everyone is saying." The hard look in his blue eyes had never been directed at me before either.

I waved that away. "I've heard that rumor too. It's probably just because we kissed and left the dance together."

His expression didn't soften. "I've heard the same rumor from everyone, and it's very specific. They're saying that you're the one who said that we hooked up. They're saying that's what you do, just hook up with guys."

"So that's why all these guys are asking me out." Two more guys had approached me today, and they had never paid any attention to me before.

"Why the hell else do you think that Dylan would ask you out? He's only after one thing. I heard you're going on a date with him. Congratulations, Cam. He'll give you what you want." His voice sounded more hurt than angry now.

"It's not a date," I clarified. "We're just hanging out, and I'm not going to have sex with him. I hardly know him!"

"A lot of girls didn't plan on having sex with him, but they did anyway. He doesn't have that reputation for nothing." Jake didn't look quite as angry now. "I don't know what this is all about, Cam, but the rumors will just get worse if you go with him to that party."

"I don't care what people say about me. It's not like I'm worried about being popular like Madison," I said.

Jake immediately went on the defensive. "So you're going to keep throwing that in my face."

"I wasn't. I didn't even know it was her until she apologized yesterday," I admitted. "Speaking of which, you never actually apologized to me about that."

Jake's eyes had narrowed. "You talked to Madison? What exactly did you say to her?"

"Just that she had the wrong idea about us kissing. I told her it meant nothing." As soon as the words were out of my mouth, I wished that I could take them back. The wounded look on Jake's face made me feel awful. "I didn't mean it like that. You know that I wanted you to kiss me."

"Yeah, whatever." His expression became neutral. "So you gave Madison the impression that we hooked up casually?"

I remembered her asking me if it was a casual thing, now that I thought about it. "She misunderstood what I said."

"Why would you tell her anything?" Jake asked in annoyance. "You know that all she does is gossip."

"That's not all she does." My tone was so unexpectedly bitter that he glanced at me sharply and kept his gaze on me.

I was suddenly uncomfortable with the keen way he was studying me. "I have to go eat before lunch is over."

I threw open the door and scampered out of the car before he could reply. He was still watching me when I looked back at him. I gave him a hesitant little wave, and he waved back. It was amazing how such a small gesture could lift my spirits so much.

Chapter 9

I wasn't sure how I got talked into going shopping with Kayla, the girl who was having the party, and her best friend. How Kyle ended up going with us was beyond me. I was asking him for advice on how to get out of it at lunch, which we were finally eating in the cafeteria, and instead of helping me he managed to get himself invited to go with us. I was sure that he only wanted to watch my torture.

Kayla and Jennifer made me shop for two hours before we finally agreed on "acceptable" clothes. I had to try everything on and model it for them. My usual clothes shopping took about fifteen minutes, and that included standing in line at the register. When I walked out in the first thing they picked out for me, all three of them stared at me. I had never before tried on a miniskirt in my life. None of my friends had ever seen me in a dress or skirt, and I wasn't planning on wearing one now.

"Darling!" Kyle cried. "You look fabulous!"

"She looks hot," Kayla said. "Cameron, I didn't know you had such a nice figure. Why do you wear all those boy clothes?"

"I'm not wearing this to the party." I was still looking at Kyle and trying to figure out what he was up to. He had never used the words darling or fabulous before to my recollection. As the shopping/torture continued, he would repeatedly call me darling and tell me that I looked fabulous. I eventually caught on that he was playing into Kayla and Jennifer's stereotypes about gay guys.

After I refused to consider skirts as a possibility, they decided that I should wear jeans. Kayla was stunned after she asked me what size jeans I wore, and I told her that I didn't know because I didn't have any. She and Jennifer exchanged a look of disbelief. Then I had to try on dozens of jeans until we found the perfect pair.

"They're too tight," I complained.

"No, they're not. You're just used to wearing baggy clothes," Kayla said.

"Darling, you look fabulous."

I shot Kyle a murderous look. By this time, I was tired and annoyed, and I regretted ever agreeing to go to this stupid party. Kayla and Jennifer picked out some girly top for me to wear with the jeans. I barely glanced at it, because I just wanted to be done shopping.

"Now for the makeup," Kayla said. "I'm guessing you don't have any."

"Forget it," I said. "Thanks for your help, but I've had it with fashion."

"Just lipstick. That's all you need. Every girl looks better with lipstick," Jennifer insisted.

"Yes, darling. All you need is a fabulous shade of lipstick." Kyle fluttered his lashes at me.

"And you need a new vocabulary, darling," I said in a falsely sweet voice.

A wicked gleam in his angelic blue eyes warned me that he was going to annoy me even worse. "What about lingerie, darling? Surely you're not going to wear boxer shorts on your date."

Kayla and Jennifer both gasped and looked horrified. For the record, I didn't wear boys' underwear. I had sensible girls cotton panties. Sure, Kyle had never seen me in my underwear, but I suspected he knew that even I wasn't going to wear boys' underwear.

"You should get a thong," Kayla said. "Dylan loves to see a girl in a thong."

"Oh yeah," Jennifer agreed. "It drives him wild."

Kyle looked like the cat that swallowed the canary. "You ladies have firsthand knowledge of this?"

"Hell yeah," Kayla said. "Dylan's the best."

"It's true what they say," Jennifer added. "Practice really does make perfect."

"How's Jake in that department?" Kayla was looking at me with open curiosity. "You're one of the few that actually knows."

I was surprised by that statement, because I had assumed that Jake slept with lots of girls. "Let's go find the lipstick," I said, willing to submit to more shopping in order to change the subject.

I allowed them to pick out the color for me, and they chose red. "It'll make your lips pop," Kayla said.

We then made a stop in the lingerie department, but I nixed the thong idea. After taking a better look at the top they had picked out for me, I realized that I needed to buy an actual bra. The girls were looking at me like I was from another planet when I admitted that I didn't know my bra size.

Kayla made a guess by looking at me, but I had to buy a bigger size than she had predicted. My breasts looked much fuller in the regular bra than they had in my sports bra. Going to a party could not possibly be worth all this trouble, I thought. Why did so many girls think that shopping was fun? Fortunately, Kyle and I had driven separately from the girls, because they decided to stay at the mall awhile longer.

Kyle waited until we were out of sight of them before he began laughing at me. "Didn't you have a fabulous time darling?"

"What the hell is wrong with you? It was bad enough without you making it worse. If you call me darling one more time, I won't be responsible for my actions," I warned him.

He was still getting a kick out of it. "The look on your face! You looked like you were being put through the Inquisition instead of just trying on clothes. At least you have something decent to wear
now. Maybe next time you'll get a skirt."

"There will be no next time," I declared. "I don't ever want to see another mall as long as I live."

"Remember, Cam, prom is next year." Kyle stepped through the door to the parking lot and held it open for me.

"Who says I'm going to prom?" I shifted the purse strap uncomfortably on my shoulder. It was the same one I'd had for years, but I rarely used it. Most of the time my pockets sufficed for carrying what I needed, but I hadn't been sure how much money to take with me, and I didn't want to have a wad of cash in my pocket.

"I thought this was a new beginning for you," Kyle said. "Accepting dates, partying, shopping."

"It's not a date," I reminded him.

"You keep telling yourself that, Cam. Dylan didn't ask you out as just a friend. All of his friends have benefits. We just went shopping with two of them, and they both gave him rave reviews. You should have taken their advice and gotten a thong."

"It's not like he'll ever see it anyway. I'm not going to have sex with him."

"I don't know," Kyle said, and he actually sounded unsure. "I hear he's very persuasive."

"He's not going to persuade me," I said confidently.

"He already persuaded you to go on a date with him," Kyle countered, ignoring my insistence that it wasn't a date.

The party was on Saturday evening, and it happened to be a night that Mom was working overtime. Connor was thrilled that I was going out, so I suspected that he would take full advantage of having the house to himself. Jake hadn't been over at all since the night of the dance. I had gotten so used to him being around that I felt his absence. We saw each other at school, and he said hi to me, but that was all.

Kyle came over on Saturday to make sure that I actually wore the new clothes I had bought. I acted affronted that he didn't trust me, even though I had been planning on wearing something comfortable. He insisted that I also put on the lipstick and leave my hair down.

"Where have you been hiding those?" He sounded mystified as he looked at my chest.

It was a combination of a bra that didn't flatten my bust and a shirt that wasn't two sizes too big. I barely recognized myself in the mirror as I stared at my reflection. The red top was a vivid color that I wasn't used to wearing. Most of my clothes were blue, white, or black.

"I take it back. You don't need the thong," Kyle joked.

Connor stopped in his tracks and stared when he saw me. "Cam? Is that you?"

"Very funny," I said.

"No, seriously. You look great! Wow. What a difference."

"What is that supposed to mean?" I asked, taking offense.

"Have fun at the party. I have to go pick up Jen." He made his escape out the front door.

"It means that you look fabulous darling." Kyle made a run for the living room as I lunged at him.

We played a video game until Dylan arrived to pick me up. He looked like he could be the hot lead singer of some rock band. His brown hair had that carelessly mussed look as it grazed his shoulders. He had a lean but not too skinny body. Dylan was every bit as attractive as Jake, although he wasn't as tall.

His dark eyes widened in surprise when he saw me, but he was too smooth to say anything about how different I looked. "Hey, Cameron. Ready to party? Hey, Kyle. How's it going man?"

He earned points with me, both for knowing Kyle's name and for treating him like he would any other guy. Kyle walked out with me, and I locked the front door before saying bye to him. Then Dylan drove me to Kayla's party. He easily made small talk with me about what kind of music I liked. True, Kayla's house turned out not to be too far away from mine, but Dylan still surprised me with how quickly he made me feel comfortable talking to him. Sure, I had never been shy around guys, but I also think that he was one of those rare people who were completely at ease with everyone.

It was a good thing that I wasn't a shy person, because I got plenty of attention when we arrived at the party. The looks of shock on people's faces when they realized who I was were almost funny. Unlike the looks of appreciation I received from other guys, Jake's expression soured as his eyes swept over me. I hadn't expected to see him at the party, and I was hurt by his reaction to my appearance.

He approached me later after Dylan excused himself to go to the bathroom. "You didn't have to bother buying new clothes, Cam. Dylan only cares about getting you out of them." He had a drink in his hand, and it wasn't his first.

Despite my resolve to ignore him and have a good time, I had been watching him drink. "You're wrong. He hasn't even tried to make a move on me." It was true. Dylan had surprised me yet again by not behaving the way his reputation had led me to believe he would.

"Yet," Jake said and took another gulp of beer.

I was still on my first drink, because I wasn't used to drinking. Jake slipped away as Dylan returned. He talked me into dancing with him, and I lost track of Jake. Even though everybody else was grinding, Dylan didn't make contact with my body as he moved with me in a subtly sensual way. It was actually sexier than if he had been right up against me.

I started to fall under his seductive spell over the course of the evening. He never once said anything suggestive, but his intimate manner let me know that he was interested. We were at a crowded party, but he managed to make it seem like it was just the two of us with his attentive focus on me. The couch we were sitting on was like our own little island in a sea of people. When he casually leaned in to kiss me, I didn't pull away.
If Jake had never kissed me, I would have thought that Dylan's kiss was perfection. The boy knew how to kiss, that was

for sure. I responded to him as he set all my hormones flooding through my body with his hot kiss. Yet there was something missing, and it worried me. I now understood what Kyle had meant when he said that your body can respond to the right stimulation, but the spark is missing.

When I broke off the kiss and pulled back, I noticed Jake standing nearby and watching us. His expression darkened even more when he saw me looking at him. He downed his drink and crushed the plastic cup in his hand before pushing his way through the crowd and toward the front door. I took off after him, leaving a startled Dylan behind.

I ran outside and yelled Jake's name to make him stop and turn toward me. Then I jumped straight at him. The drinks he'd consumed had slowed his reflexes, so I was able to tackle him to the ground and land on top of him. He grunted with the impact, and his eyes opened wide in surprise as I groped at him.

"What the fuck?" He angrily pushed me off him, but I had already fished his car keys out of his pocket.

I was up in a flash and running toward his car, pressing the alarm to help me find it. Jake would have caught up to me faster with his long legs if he hadn't been drunk. I made it into the car and snapped my seatbelt into place. He leaned in and tried to unbuckle it. "Get out!"

"You're too drunk to drive," I argued.

He hit his head on the roof of the car during the struggle. "Ow!"

Jake pulled his body back out of the car and rubbed his sore head. He glared at Dylan, who was standing beside the car and watching us with obvious amusement.

"Jake," I yelled. "Get in the damn car!"

He stomped around to the passenger side and yanked the door open. Then he eased himself carefully onto the seat, wary of hitting his head again.

"Do you need any help?" Dylan asked.

"No thanks," I said. "I've got this."

"I was talking to Jake," he said with his signature sexy laugh.

"Drive," Jake growled.

"Bye, Cameron. It was a pleasure," Dylan said as he shut the door for me.

Jake loudly slammed his door, and I drove away. He didn't say a word until I pulled into my driveway and took his keys with me as I exited the car. He came charging out of the car as I unlocked the front door and rushed into the house.

"Damn it, Cam. Give me back my keys!" He was inside now, so I closed the door.

"You're staying here tonight," I said calmly. Then I turned and sprinted up the stairs.

I heard him swear as he followed me, and I prayed that he wouldn't trip and fall. Fortunately, he made it up safely and caught up to me in the hallway. "I wanna go home." Now he sounded like a little kid complaining.

"Tomorrow," I said as I put my arm around his waist and walked him into my room. "You haven't been here all week."

"That's because it's killing me to be around you." The sudden raw pain in his voice tugged at my heart.

"It'll be okay," I soothed. "Let's get you comfortable." I took a steadying breath and undid the button on his jeans before sliding the zipper down. I heard him inhale sharply, but I tried to remain brisk and efficient as I removed his jeans. He was sitting on my bed now, and I pulled the jeans the rest of the way off his legs. "Okay, go to sleep."

He obediently lay down and closed his eyes. I turned my back to him and removed my own clothes, except for my panties, and put on my pajamas. When I turned around, Jake's eyes were open and watching me in a way that made me catch my breath. Then he turned on his side, and I turned off the light and got into bed beside him. Everything was silent except for our soft breathing. Eventually, I began to drift slowly toward sleep.

"I love you, Cam," Jake murmured.

My eyes flew open in the darkness, but he didn't speak again. Within minutes, his steady, even breathing revealed that he was asleep. Slumber eluded me for a long time after as I was filled with a strange elation.

Chapter 10

Jake and I had gone to sleep with our backs turned to each other, but I woke the next morning with his body warm against my back and his arm draped over my waist. I didn't know if he was awake yet, but a certain part of his anatomy sure was. With our bodies pressed so close together, I could definitely feel it.

Then I realized that the stupid buttons on my pajama top had popped open again. Only the bottom two buttons were holding it together, and my breasts were spilling out of it. I had meant to buy new pajamas when I went shopping, but I had forgotten about it in my annoyance at having to try on so many jeans. I made a move to button my top, but Jake's hand lifted from my waist and covered my hand to stop me. There was no doubt now that he was awake. Heat spread through my body in anticipation of his touch as I dropped my hand to give him access.

"I just want to look at you," he whispered in my ear, sending my temperature soaring even more.

After a couple more minutes, he pulled away from me and shifted his body to get off the bed. He grabbed his jeans off the floor and sat back down on the bed to put them on. We couldn't really talk for fear of waking Mom, so Jake turned to take another lingering look at me before he eased the door open to step out into the hallway.

He shut it quietly behind him, and I sat up and swung my legs over the side of the bed. I unbuttoned the other two buttons on my pajama top and took off my pajamas. I got dressed and peeked out into the hallway. The door to the bathroom was open, so Jake must have gone downstairs. Connor's bedroom door was closed, and he was probably still sleeping.

After I was done in the bathroom, I went downstairs and found Jake in the kitchen. We could speak in hushed voices down here. He asked me if I wanted him to make me something for breakfast.

"I'll just throw some waffles in the toaster," I said. "Do you want some too?"

"No thanks. I'm not hungry." He took the waffles out of the freezer and popped them in the toaster for me.

"Hangover?" I asked.

"No, I didn't drink that much." He took a plate out of the cabinet for me. "I drank enough not to be okay to drive though. Thanks for stopping me."

I grabbed the butter and syrup out of the fridge. "Yeah, I couldn't let you take a chance like that."

"I'm sorry about the way I acted last night, Cam. I had no right to say that to you."

I had been about to sit down, but now I stood looking at the kitchen table. "Why not? If that's how you feel…"

He set two glasses on the counter and turned to look at me. "I was being an idiot. That's not really how I feel." The waffles popped up from the toaster, and he picked up the plate and walked over to it.

"So, you don't love me?"

He froze in the process of reaching for the waffles. "What?" His back was still turned to me as he spoke.

I walked over to look at him. "Last night you said that you love me."

He was staring at the toaster instead of looking at me. "When? I don't remember that."

"It was right before you fell asleep. Is it true, Jake? Do you love me?" After he left my room, my mind had immediately returned to the last words he had spoken to me last night.

"I was drunk," he said as he removed the waffles from the toaster.

I watched him set the plate down on the kitchen table for me. He asked me what I wanted to drink, and I chose milk with my waffles. He poured himself a glass of water and took a few gulps.

"I was talking about what I said to you at the party. It's none of my business what you do with Dylan." He picked up Connor's car keys. "Where are my keys?"

"They're still in my jeans pocket. You're not leaving yet, are you?" The morning had started off so great, but I was disappointed with the way things were turning out.

"Yeah, I should get home. I didn't even tell my parents that I was staying over. You go ahead and eat. I'll go get the keys."

"No," I said. "I'll get them. There's no way to explain it if Mom sees you with your hand in my pants."

Jake laughed, and I reached out to cover his mouth. "Shh! You'll wake up Mom. Anyway, you know what I meant."

At the touch of my hand, his laughter stopped. I dropped my hand, but I couldn't look away from his suddenly heated gaze. He was the one who broke eye contact. "Do you mind getting my keys, Cam?"

With deepening disappointment, I left him standing in the kitchen and went upstairs to get his keys. He was worried about my breakfast getting cold, and he wanted to move Connor's car by himself, but I insisted on helping him. I pulled back into the driveway after he backed his car out and took off down the street.

Feeling unusually lonely, I ate my breakfast by myself as I stared at Jake's glass on the countertop. He had seemed intent on keeping me company until I had mentioned what he said to me last night. He hadn't even remembered saying it, but he had been upset by it. His entire demeanor had changed when I had questioned him about it.

I didn't understand his reaction, but I understood my own even less. Last night I had been inexplicably happy to hear him tell me that, and now I felt let down at hearing him say that it wasn't true. Did I want him to be in love with me? If I was honest with myself, I had to admit that the thought appealed to me. The question now was why?

Connor walked into the kitchen and interrupted my thoughts. We said good morning to each other, and I toasted some waffles for him. I soon noticed that the atmosphere between us was wrong too. He seemed to be avoiding looking directly at me.

I waited until he had finished his breakfast. "What's going on with you?"

"Not here." He stood up and motioned for me to follow him. Then he stopped at the bottom of the stairs and listened. He was obviously trying to hear if Mom was up yet. Seemingly satisfied that she wasn't, he led me toward the basement and down the steps.

I rarely ventured down here anymore, but I had often spied on Connor and Jake when we were kids. Connor went through a no girls allowed phase, and I had delighted in annoying him. I looked toward the bar, and I was reminded of something that happened when we were twelve.

My parents had never kept liquor down here, but they hadn't bothered to remove the bar the previous owner had left behind. On this particular day, it was my hiding place for the prank I was about to pull on Connor and Jake. I laid in wait with several water balloons. Sure, I would get in trouble for throwing them in the house, but it would be worth it to piss off Connor. Jake was just an innocent bystander, but it was his fault for not having better taste in friends. Besides, he never held a grudge against me. Connor would get mad, but Jake would laugh about it.

I heard them coming down the steps and prepared to launch my attack, but I got distracted by their conversation. "You're lying," Jake said.

"No, I swear it's true. I kissed Stephanie," Connor insisted.

"On the lips?" Jake asked skeptically.

"Of course on the lips. It was, it was…" Words seemed to fail Connor. "It was good," he finally finished. "You gotta try it."

"With Stephanie?" Jake teased.

"No, get your own girl! Maybe Nicole or somebody. Who do you think is pretty?" Connor asked.

"Cam," Jake said.

"Cam? You mean my sister?" Connor's voice was equal parts shock and horror.

"Yeah," Jake confirmed. "She's the prettiest girl."

"Cam?" Connor laughed. "She doesn't even look like a girl. The prettiest girl is Ashley."

"Ashley has the prettiest hair," Jake said.

"Yeah," Connor agreed. "The prettiest girls are blonde."

"No, not the color. I just like how long it is. There's just something about long hair."

My own hair was boyishly short. I had never before thought about how it looked. My only concern had been with keeping it out of my face while I played sports. It had been strange to hear Jake say that I was pretty.

I stayed hidden behind that bar until Jake and Connor decided to go outside. My legs fell asleep from sitting on the floor for so long, and I seriously had to go pee. I waited until Jake went home before I let loose on Connor with the water balloons. As weeks went by Mom was surprised when she noticed that I was growing out my hair.

I was stunned by the realization that I had grown my hair long because Jake had said that he liked long hair. Why had I cared about what he liked?

"Don't look so shocked, Cam. Did you really think I wouldn't figure it out when I saw his car was here?" Connor asked now.

"What?" I had been lost in my memories and missed what he had been talking about.

"He had to sleep somewhere, and the only place I didn't check was your room." Connor was obviously upset about that.

"So what?" I challenged.

"So what? You told me that you're not having sex with him." His voice was hushed but angry.

"I'm not," I said.

"C'mon, Cam. Do you expect me to believe that he spent all night in your bed, and nothing happened?"

I was pissed off now. "Excuse me, but how is this your business? Do I worry about what goes on in your room? Don't try to play big brother with me, because we're the same age."

Connor backed off a little. "It's just weird for me to think of my best friend hooking up with my sister."

"We didn't hook up. Jake had too much to drink at the party, and I didn't want him to drive home drunk. So I brought him here to sleep it off," I explained.

He still didn't look convinced. "And why exactly did he have to sleep it off in your room?"
"After what happened last time, I wasn't setting foot in your room. How did I know that you weren't planning to have your girlfriend spend the night?" It all sounded reasonable when I said it, but I couldn't fool myself that it was the complete truth.

"I drove Jen home, and I was surprised when I saw Jake's car here. He hasn't wanted to come over at all since you guys went to that dance. Look, Cam, I don't really want to know the details, but did you guys make up?"

"We're cool," I said, but I wasn't so sure.

Chapter 11

I missed Jake. It was a subtle, gradual realization over the next few weeks. He never returned to our house after he spent the night in my room. When Connor hung out with him now, it was always at Jake's house or elsewhere. Jake no longer came to watch my soccer games like he had in the past. He spoke to me at school, but only to say hi. I had taken his presence for granted for so long that I wasn't prepared for how much being cut out of his life would affect me.

I didn't tell anyone what he had said to me that night when he was drunk, not even Kyle. Jake had said that it wasn't true, and there was no reason to dwell on it. Kyle and I had other things to deal with. The rest of our friends seemed to always be busy whenever we wanted to hang out. I decided to confront them about it, starting with Adam. He was surprised when I took the school bus home with him. I stuck to small talk until we got off the bus.

"How are you going to get home?" Adam asked. "You know I don't have a car."

I knew that his parents didn't get home from work until about six, so we could talk openly at his house. "I can call Connor to pick me up. Or maybe Kyle," I added.

Adam looked away from me as we walked into his yard. He seemed reluctant to invite me in, but he did anyway. "So, what do you want to do?" We hadn't ever hung out together without the rest of our friends, and he seemed kind of nervous around me, although he never had been before.

"I want to talk, or are you too busy?" I had dropped the friendly tone of voice I'd used on the bus.

"Just don't punch me, okay?" He actually stepped back away from me.

"Why would I do that, Adam? I still consider you my friend. Or am I wrong about that?" I wondered if this was going to be a replay of what happened with Chad.

"Of course we're still friends, Cam. You're not the problem," he said.

My anger dissolved into disappointment. "What is the problem then, Adam?" I already knew, but I wanted to make him say it.

"Let me ask you something, Cam. How long have you known about Kyle being gay?" At least he was looking straight at me now instead of avoiding the situation.

"A couple of years. Obviously, I didn't drop him as a friend when I found out."

"I don't know how he told you, but he just sprang it on us with no warning. Give me some time to get used to it," he said.

"You're not going to get used to it by avoiding him. He's still the same person, Adam. Nothing has to change. Just give him a chance," I pleaded.

"I don't know what to say to him," he admitted.

"You don't have to say anything. We'll just hang out like always. Okay?"

"Okay, Cam, but I don't know if it can be like it was before. Have you talked to the other guys yet?" Adam asked.

"Not yet, but I'm actually going over to talk to Jason now. I texted him during last period, and he said he'd be home." Jason lived a couple blocks over from Adam, so I could walk there.

"Oh." His tone of voice immediately alerted me that something was wrong.

"What? Did he say something awful about Kyle?" Jason had always been so cool about everything that I couldn't imagine him reacting in the way Chad did. Yet I hadn't expected Chad to behave that way either.

"No. We haven't really talked about Kyle at all. I guess we just wanted to pretend it never happened," Adam explained. "Did you know that Jason was at Kayla's party?"

The abrupt change of subject puzzled me, but I answered him. "No, I didn't see him."

"He saw you."

There was something odd about the way he said that. "Oh? Why didn't he say hi?"

"Maybe because he was too busy drooling over you." He watched my reaction and smiled thinly. "Yeah, I couldn't believe it either. All he could talk about was how hot you looked. You should know that he's been trying to work up the nerve to ask you out."

"Oh no!" Why was this happening to me?

"Are you still going to go talk to him?" Adam asked.

"Yes. Our friendship is too important to just give up on it. I don't know why everything is so complicated though."

"Yeah," he agreed. "Things were much easier when we were kids."

"Those were the days," I sighed.

He smiled, and I could see the Adam I had always known. "Listen to us talking about the good old days."

I smiled back. "We must be getting old."

"Ancient." Then he grew serious again. "Come back here and wait for your ride if things get too
weird with Jason."

"Thanks, Adam." I left his house feeling hopeful. He was open to trying to keep our friendships intact.
My optimism even carried over to the situation with Jason. I was dressed in my usual clothes, and I felt confident that he would forget about the party once he saw me. Surely one evening wouldn't override all the years we had been buddies. He dispelled that hope quickly, however. I had launched into talking to him about Kyle, but he interrupted me.

"I'm sorry, Cam, but there's something I need to say to you before I freeze up. I like you, and I want to know if you'll go out with me."

Why was my life such a mess? "Since when do you like me, Jason? Since you saw how hot I looked?" I was angrier at the situation than I was at him.

"Adam and his big mouth," he muttered. "Yeah, Cam, I couldn't help noticing your looks. I know there's more to you than your body though. We have a lot in common. I never thought about you as more than a friend before, and maybe you've never thought about me that way either, but I think we could have something special."

We had been friends for a long time, and I didn't want to suspect him of ulterior motives, but I had to bring it up. "A lot of guys have been asking me out lately, Jason. If you think—"

He looked offended as he jumped in to deny it before I even said it. "I saw you were at the party with Dylan, and I've heard the rumors about you, but I know you're not that kind of girl. You're my friend first. How could you think that I would try to use you?"

"You had a date at the dance," I reminded him.

"Yeah I date, Cam, but I don't have a girlfriend. Not yet anyway. Will you please think about it? About going out with me, I mean."

He was right about us having a lot in common. Besides our love of skateboarding, we also had the same taste in music and movies. We got along great, and Jason was attractive. He was just as blond as Kyle, but he had brown eyes. I was noticing his looks for the first time since my late blooming hormones had kicked in. Still, I wished that we could just go back to our effortless friendship.

"I promise to think about it if you'll hang out with Kyle and me the way you used to before the dance." I wasn't just making a false promise to bribe him. I was really going to consider everything he said.

He knew me well enough to take me at my word. I didn't go around breaking promises. "Okay, Cam, you've got a deal. Do you want me to talk to Kevin and Taylor for you?"

"Yeah," I said gratefully. "That would be great."

"Okay, I'll let you know and we'll get together if they're cool with it." Before I knew what was happening, Jason leaned in and lightly brushed his lips against mine. "You let me know too, Cam."

"I will," I promised. Then I decided to take Adam up on his offer. "I told Connor to pick me up at Adam's house," I lied. "I better get going."
I made my escape and called Connor when I turned the corner and was no longer visible from Jason's house. I had made progress with my goal to help ease the rift between Kyle and the rest of my friends, but now I had a new problem to solve.

Chapter 12

I couldn't seem to get away from the whole dating thing, even though I had wanted nothing to do with it. It was like a virus that had infected everyone, and now they were spreading it to me. It had started with Jake. Everything could be traced back to Jake in my mind. He was responsible for all these confusing feelings I now had.

My life had been simple and uncomplicated until he stimulated my hormones into going crazy for him. He was the one who set off this entire chain of events that had messed up my life. It was because of him that I had agreed to go to the party with Dylan where Jason had seen me and decided that he wanted to be more than friends. Now I was in the awkward situation of having to decide what to do about Jason.

My first impulse would be to tell him that I wanted to remain just friends, but I had promised to think about it. Dating Jason would be easy. We liked so many of the same things that we would always agree on what to do on our dates. The only difference in our relationship would be the kissing. I had to admit that I liked kissing, so it would be nice to have someone to kiss on a regular basis.

I had told Jake that I didn't want to date anyone, so he would be hurt if I started dating Jason after refusing him. So far, I had liked kissing Jake more than I liked kissing anyone else. If I was going to date anyone for the kissing, he would be the natural choice.

Yet I felt afraid of getting involved with him that way. Even Dylan seemed like a safer choice for dating. He had made it clear that he was still interested and told me to call him anytime if I wanted to go out again. I wasn't even sure if Jake still wanted me to be his girlfriend, or if he had gotten over me like he said he would.

It was obvious to me now that he had liked me since we were kids. What freaked me out was the possibility that I had liked him all along too. How else could I explain to myself why I had grown my hair long for him? I had told him that having sex with him would make me stop thinking of him as more than a friend, but now I wasn't so sure. If my feelings for him predated the incident in my room, then they weren't going to go away by trying to exorcise the physical attraction between us. His absence should have made it easier to put him out of my mind, but I was feeling it more keenly with every passing week. I wondered if he missed me the way I missed him. He had said that being around me was killing him, so maybe he was glad to be away from me.

Kyle told me that dating Jason would only lead to disaster. "Your heart's not in it, Cam. If he starts falling for you, you'll only break his heart. Then your friendship will be ruined."

Was that why I hadn't been scared when Jason asked me out, because I knew I was safe from heartbreak with him? What did that say about my reaction to Jake? I remembered my panic when he asked me if I returned his feelings. I was starting to come to a conclusion I didn't like.

I pushed those thoughts to the back of my mind as I prepared to hang out with my friends. Jason had texted me that we were on for skateboarding with all the guys. We were taking advantage of the weather before it got too cold. I had made my decision about Jason, but I was going to tell him when we were alone. Kyle and I were driving separately to the skate park so that I could talk to Jason afterward. I was nervous about it, but I was more nervous about how the guys would treat Kyle.

It was a little awkward at first when we all greeted each other, but having an activity to distract us really helped. We were soon having fun skateboarding and attempting to perfect our moves. Kyle flawlessly pulled off a trick that had always thwarted him before, and we all cheered for him.

It was when he and Adam got into an argument about zombies, however, that I felt like things were back to normal. The rest of the guys joined in with their own opinions on this pointless disagreement. As I listened to them, I felt my heart swell with happiness. We were going to be okay.

Once things started winding down when everybody was going home for dinner, I hung back with Jason. He picked up on my cues that I wanted to talk, and he stayed with me after everybody else left.

"Seems like everybody's cool with him," Jason said.

"Yeah, thanks for setting this up. Did you have trouble talking Kevin and Taylor into coming?"

"They weren't exactly thrilled about it," he admitted. "I think we were all worried it was going to be weird, but it was like old times."

"They just needed to see that he's still Kyle. It's not like he suddenly became a different person."

"That would actually have been an improvement," Jason joked.

I laughed, but I was already dreading the next part of our conversation. "So, I thought about what you said. Our friendship is important to me, Jason, and I don't want to lose it."

"It's important to me too, Cam. If things don't work out with dating, we can still be friends."

"I think we should just stay friends." Kyle was right. I really had no desire to start a romance with Jason.

He looked disappointed. "So, you just don't like me that way."

"I'm sorry, Jason." I was worried about where we would go from here, because I could tell that he was unhappy with my answer.

"No, it's okay. Anyway, I gotta go. I'll see you at school." He took off without me then, even though we were going to the same parking area.

I let him have his space as I walked slowly back to the car with my skateboard. Jason had never shown any romantic interest in me before, so I hoped he would get over this soon.

Kyle seemed to think so. "He's just hot for you, Cam. He'll move on to lusting after some other
girl. What about Jake? Anything new going on with him?"

I had nothing to report. Kyle would make a big deal out of it, so I didn't tell him that I had gone to see Jake play basketball. Connor was on the team too, but my motivation had been seeing Jake. It wasn't just his gorgeous looks either. I missed Jake, and I had thought about letting him know that I was there but had ended up just sitting inconspicuously on the bleachers and watching the game. We lost, and Jake's mood seemed even worse than that of the rest of his team.

That was the only time I saw him outside of school until the day of the funeral. My mom's cousin died, and Mom insisted that Connor and I had to go even though we had only seen the woman at family reunions and barely remembered her. She had lived in a town two hours away from us, so it was going to waste most of our Saturday, I thought ungraciously.

"Wow! Check out those houses," Connor said as we drove through a residential area on our way to the cemetery.

"Candace married into money," Mom told us. "Not that it was the reason she married Edward," she quickly amended. "They met in college and fell in love."

It was true, because Candace's husband was clearly grieving for her. Their kids were all grown, but I could tell they were close to their dad as they all cried for their mom. The whole thing was sad, and I was glad when it was over. After I awkwardly took my turn in giving them my condolences, I spotted Jake standing in another section of the cemetery. I looked again, and it was definitely him. What was he doing here?

I motioned to Mom where I was going, and she nodded and continued talking to another relative I didn't know. Connor was talking to some girl and didn't notice me walk away. Jake was as surprised to see me as I was to see him. "What are you doing here?" We had both asked the question at the same time.

"My dad and grandpa are buried here," he said.

"What?" How could Connor fail to tell me that Jake's dad died?

He saw my horrified expression. "My other dad, Cam. He died a long time ago."

Now I was thoroughly confused. "What other dad?"

"My mom was only married to him for a year. I was a baby when they got divorced, and he died when I was two. I don't remember him at all, but I come up here once in a while."

I was shocked to learn this. He had never mentioned it in all the years that I'd known him. I looked down at the headstone. "You have his last name."

"Yeah, I'm the last of the family. My dad was an only child, and he only had me," Jake said.

"Cam," Connor called. "Hey, Jake." He turned back to me. "Mom says we have to go to the wake   now. I guess they're having food and stuff."

"Jake said he'd drive me home." I knew Jake well enough to be sure that he wouldn't contradict me.

"Yeah," Jake said, proving me right.

"Hold on. I'll go talk to Mom." I started to walk away then turned back to Connor. "Do you want me to get you out of it too?"

"No, that's okay. I'll keep Mom company on the ride back."

He squirmed under my disapproving glare. "Are you seriously trying to pick up a girl at a funeral? What about Jen?"

"I'm just talking to Ashley," Connor said defensively.

"Another damn Ashley," I muttered as I walked toward Mom.

To my dismay, her mom radar zeroed in on my situation with Jake. "Is he the guy?"

"Yeah," I confirmed while looking at my feet.

"I thought so," Mom said, making me look up at her in astonishment.

"As much as I love his cooking, he wasn't doing it for me."

I wondered what she meant by that. "So, can I go? Please?"

"Okay," she said. "We'll talk later."

Connor had filled Jake in on why we were there, and Jake asked me if I wanted to stop somewhere to get something to eat.

"We can stop if you're hungry." I was still waiting for him to say something about me inviting myself to ride home with him.

"I'd rather wait until we get back." He put the keys in the ignition but didn't turn on the car. His smile was warm when he looked at me. "Where are we going, Cam?"

I, too, had been thinking of our childhood game. It started one morning when I got up before everyone else. I grabbed a box of cereal and went into the garage. Mom always parked her car in the garage. Even now, we always parked over to the side of the driveway so she could pull into the garage. Back then, hers was the only car after she and my dad got divorced. I got in and pretended to drive as I munched on dry cereal. Jake found me there and got in the passenger seat. Connor would always fight with me about who got to "drive."

Jake grabbed a handful of cereal. "Where are we going, Cam?"
I decided on Texas, because that sounded like a lot of fun to me. We really got into it as we made up all kinds of adventures about what we were doing in Texas. Somehow, there were cowboys and Indians even though we were in a modern car.

"I want to drive," Connor demanded when he finally got up and found us.

I left them to go get dressed and play with my friends. It became our special thing, however. In those days, Jake only slept over on the weekend, and we had a babysitter on the nights Mom worked. Those weekend mornings became my special time with Jake.

We traveled all over the country, and I started looking things up so that I could add more places to our adventures. One time we went to Myrtle Beach, and I spoke about it from memory. It was my most treasured family vacation, because it was before Dad's drinking got out of control. I started off excitedly taking Jake to the beach with me and sharing all the things I remembered doing there. Then I started to get sad and stopped talking. I hated crying, and I squeezed my eyes shut angrily.

"Let's go to Japan," Jake said.

I gave him a watery smile. "We can't drive across the ocean."

"We can. There's a secret tunnel at the bottom, and you can drive anywhere in the world."

This fired up my imagination. "Yeah, let's go. I want to go to Japan."

"I was there once with my grandpa," he said.

My tears were forgotten as I stared at him. "You went to Japan? Did you drive through the tunnel?" I thought he had made up the tunnel, but I wasn't sure.

"No, we went on a plane. But we'll take the tunnel there now."

I was jealous, because I had never flown on a plane. Once we started traveling the world, our imaginations came up with unlimited journeys. We even decided to time travel at one point. The game continued well past when we should have been too old to play it. Sometimes we just sat in Mom's car and talked. I would tell him about something hilarious that had happened to one of my friends, and Jake would tell me funny stories about his brothers and sisters. The game ended when we were twelve, shortly before I overheard him telling Connor that I was pretty.

It was hot, and our air conditioner wasn't able to cool the house down enough for me to be comfortable in my pajamas, so I put on the thin nightgown Mom had bought for me but I had never worn. It kept me cool, because there wasn't much material to it. It was short and only thin straps covered my shoulders. Jake was drinking a glass of milk when I walked into the kitchen, and he started coughing.

I whacked him on the back, even though he couldn't really choke on liquid. "Went down the wrong pipe, huh?"

"I'm okay." He turned away from me, even though he was still talking to me. "Want me to make you breakfast?" By this time, I was aware of his skill in the kitchen.

"No thanks. I'm going for a ride." I walked past him and opened the cabinet to get a glass. I could feel the nightgown ride up as I reached for a glass. When I turned around, Jake was staring at me. "What?" I asked

.

"Nothing. Want some juice?" His voice was in the process of changing. Maybe that was why it sounded funny.

"Yeah." I set my glass on the counter while he took a carton of orange juice out of the fridge. "Thanks," I said after he filled my glass. I took a big gulp of it before setting it down on the counter. Mom would kill me if I spilled it in her new car, so I left it there for later. I licked the juice off my lips and swiped a hand over my mouth.

Jake was silent as he followed me out to the car. I slipped on my flip-flops before stepping out into the garage. Jake stepped into his tennis shoes. We took our usual places in the car. "Where are you gonna go when you get your own car?" I asked.

"Where do you want to go, Cam?"

"I meant for real, Jake. Where do you want to go when you get a car?" After all the places we had pretended to go, I was curious where he would pick to go in real life.

"Wherever you want to go, Cam. As long as I can really drive there." He smiled, probably remembering the imaginary tunnel at the bottom of the ocean.

"You'll take me with you?" I was pleased that he was including me in his future plans.

"I'll always take you with me, Cam." His blue eyes looked kind of intense then.

"Can we go without Connor?" I asked to lighten the mood.

"Connor who?" Jake joked.

"I know," I said, seized with sudden inspiration. "We'll be bank robbers."

He was looking at me like I had lost my mind. "That's what you want to do when I get my car?"

“No, silly, now. Okay, the cops are after us. We need a hostage. You be the hostage.”

“How can I be the bank robber and the hostage?” Jake asked.

“We’ll pretend that bank robber you is driving. I want to be the one holding the gun.” I climbed over into his lap and held my hand up to his head like a gun.

“Cam,” he said desperately, “get off.” His voice cracked as he spoke.

“Shut up,” I said, getting into my role. “Don’t give us any trouble, and we might let you live.”

Jake was looking at me in a way I had never seen before. I didn’t know what that expression was, but it kind of mesmerized me for a minute. This close up, I noticed that he was starting to sweat, even though he was only wearing his boxer shorts. My discomfort snapped me out of my trance. “You have a rock in your shorts,” I stated.

I didn’t know why he would be embarrassed by that. Rocks came in handy for pranks and for defending yourself against bullies. Plus, they were just fun to throw at things. Jake, however, looked so embarrassed that he was turning red. “I have to go to the bathroom.” He sounded almost like he was in pain.
“I climbed off him and back into the driver’s seat. “Okay, I’ll hold off the cops until you get back.”

He never came back though. After a while, I got bored and went into the house. Jake was sitting at the kitchen table with Connor. "It was too hot," he said in answer to my questioning look.

I shrugged and drank the rest of my juice.

"I didn't know it was Halloween," Connor said. "Nice costume, Cam, but you still don't look like a girl." He laughed at his own lame joke.

I looked curiously at Jake, who was flushing in embarrassment again. "Wanna play video games, Connor?"

"Yeah, it's too hot to go outside." Connor finished eating his cereal, and they went down into the basement.

I was a little hurt that Jake hadn't asked me to play too. He always had before, even though I usually opted not to hang out with Connor. I took out a bowl and poured myself some milk and cereal. Oh well, I didn't want to play with them anyway.

It turned out that Jake didn't want to hang out in Mom's car with me anymore either. He would busy himself in the kitchen making breakfast for us. We still talked, but we had to speak in hushed voices in the house. Our time in the car had been more private and fun, but I guessed that he had become bored with our silly games.

"Oh," I said now, realizing what had happened back then.

"What?" Jake asked.

"I was just thinking about the last time we hung out in Mom's car. Do you remember that?"

"I'll never forget it. That was the highlight of my preteen life," he said with a smile.

"I really thought it was a rock," I said, laughing at my cluelessness.

"The best part is that it took you this long to figure out that it wasn't," Jake laughed. "Only you, Cam. Only you." He turned on the ignition and started driving toward the cemetery exit.

"You know," I said. "We never took that trip you promised me we would after you got your car."

He glanced at me. "Do you still want to go with me, Cam?"

"Do you still want to take me?" I felt like I was asking about more than just a road trip.

"That depends, Cam. Where do you want to go?" It seemed that he, too, was also talking about more than a road trip.

Chapter 13

"How about Texas?" I asked with false enthusiasm. "That was the first place we went in Mom's car."

Jake was silent for a moment as he watched the road. "I remember."

I wondered if he was just saying that. "You do?"

"Yes, Cam. I remember all of it, all our special times together. Connor wasn't the only reason I spent so much time at your house." He pulled up to a stoplight and glanced at me.

So, we were really going to get into this. We had to drive two hours to get home, and there was no way to avoid an uncomfortable conversation about us. "I remember those times too, Jake. I always thought of you as Connor's friend, but I've realized that you were my friend too. Why don't you come over anymore?"

"Do you miss me?" His blue eyes were on me again and then refocused on the road.

I had already admitted it to myself, and now I told him the truth. "Yes, Jake, I do. I miss you so much that I even went to one of your games just so I could see you."

"I saw you there," he said. "It didn't put me in a good mood."

I was hurt by his statement. "I didn't know my presence was that intolerable to you. I'm surprised you agreed to drive me home if that's how you feel."

"You know that I would do anything for you, Cam."

He spoke the truth. I remembered when he was in my class in elementary school. The PTA sponsored an ice cream party for us, and every kid got a little cup of ice cream. I loved ice cream and wished that we could have gotten more. Jake gave me his, even though he liked ice cream too.

There were many instances like this throughout my childhood, the most significant being the one when he took the blame for me breaking the window. Just last year I had been upset about not having enough money to go to a professional skateboarding competition that I wanted to watch.

The next day I found money on my desk. It was exactly how much I had been short for the ticket. I knew that it was from Jake, but he claimed not to know anything about it. After I saved up enough money to pay him back, he refused to take it and still wouldn't admit that he had been the one to leave it for me.

"I'm still trying to get over you," he said. "I just need some distance for that. Do you understand?"

I didn't understand, because being apart from him was just making me miss him more. "Can't we
still be friends?"

"I don't know," Jake said, making my heart sink. "I don't know if I can go back to being just friends after kissing you."

I tried to make light of it. "Kyle kissed me, and he's still my friend."

Jake didn't crack a smile. "That's not the same."

"Because you love me?" My heart was hammering in my chest as I dared to call him out on this. I had my head turned to look out my window, and I didn't look at him as the silence stretched between us.

"Yes, Cam," he confirmed. "Because I love you."

I still didn't have the courage to look at him, so I continued to stare out the window until he pulled onto the highway. I knew that he was waiting for me to respond to that, but I felt frozen in a strange kind of limbo. Eventually I began to talk about everything that had been going on in my life while we had been apart. I told him about Kyle, about Jason asking me out, and even about everything that Mom had said to me about relationships.

"Cam," Jake said as I wound down my nervous chatter. "I'm sorry."

My gaze finally met his straight on before he returned his attention to the road. "About what?"

"About what you caught me doing in your room. I don't even know why I did that. Especially after what happened the first time. I couldn't believe that she still wanted to after that. You asked me how many times I used your bed. It was twice. You were at a soccer game the first time." He had barely taken a breath as he confessed all that.

I took a moment to grasp everything he had said. "What happened the first time?"

"Maybe we shouldn't get into that." He sounded even more uneasy about it now.

"You can't say something like that and leave me hanging," I protested. "It'll drive me crazy wondering about it."

"Just remember that I'm driving. We could get into an accident if you punch me."

"You punch somebody one time, and people think you make a habit out of it," I grumbled.

"I called out your name."

He glanced at me and saw my blank look. "During sex, Cam. I called out your name while I was with her."

I tried to control the emotional whirlwind that was suddenly spinning through my heart and mind.
"I was thinking about you when Dylan kissed me."

"You were?" It was the first bright smile I had seen on his face in a long time.

"Yeah, it was better with you." Since I was completely overwhelmed by all these revelations, I desperately changed the subject. "How's your family?"

Just like old times, he told me fun stories about the loving chaos that was his family. It made me want to meet them and spend some time at his house for a change. That was unlikely to ever happen now, I thought sadly. He didn't want to be my friend anymore, and he would probably go back to avoiding me after we got home. After a while, we ran out of neutral things to talk about, and Jake turned on the radio. We were both lost in our own thoughts until he pulled off the highway.

"Do you want me to take you somewhere to eat?"

Things were just too awkward between us now for me to have any appetite to eat dinner with him. "No thanks. I'm not hungry."

We were quiet again until he pulled into my driveway. Then we kind of just stared at each other.

"Where are we going, Cam?"

This time I didn't pretend to misunderstand his meaning. "I don't know, Jake. Will you give me some time to think about it?"

"Okay, but I can't be here while you decide. You come to me when you're ready. Just don't leave me hanging, Cam. Let me know one way or the other, whatever your final decision is."

"I will," I promised.

It was the same promise I had made to Jason, but this time I knew that my heart was involved in the outcome.

Chapter 14

Nobody could help me decide what to do about Jake. I talked to Mom first after she came home from the funeral. She listened to me explain that he had asked me out, and I wasn't sure what to do. "But you said that you like him," she said.

"I do, but I liked being just friends with him." I twisted her bedspread in my hands as I sat on her bed.

"And Jake wants more than that." Mom was sitting beside me. We were in her room with the door closed.

I didn't want Connor to hear this conversation, even though he knew more about the situation than Mom did. She didn't need to know about what happened in my room. "He says that he can't go back to being just friends." I looked down at my hands. "We kissed a few times."

"If you like him enough to kiss him more than once, then you must like him enough to go out with him. What's holding you back, Cam?"

"I'm afraid." This wasn't an easy thing for me to admit. When it came to physical fear, my instinct was to overcome it. "Things start off great in relationships, but then they end."

"That's not true," Mom insisted. "They don't always end."

"They do!" I cried. "You and Daddy used to be happy, but where is he now?"

"Oh, Cam." Mom hugged me.

I hugged her tight as I pulled myself back together. When our embrace ended, I was able to speak more calmly. "Don't you wish that it had never happened? That you could go back and make a different choice?"

Mom looked at me intently. "I could never wish that, Cam. Like you said, we were happy. Those memories are still with me, and I have you and Connor. I wouldn't trade that for anything."

I thought then that Mom might not be as physically strong as some people, but she had an inner strength that I admired. "But your life would have been easier in so many ways."

"Easier doesn't necessarily mean better," she said. "You know that saying about it being better to have loved and lost than never to have loved at all? I'm one of those people who believes it. I can't tell you what to do, and I can't promise you that your relationship with Jake will last. There's no way to know that. I think in your heart, though, you already know what you want."

What was in my heart? I wasn't a person who spent a lot of time contemplating my feelings. Now I had to consider what Jake meant to me. It had been nice to spend time with him again, even if the atmosphere between us hadn't exactly been comfortable. I had missed him, and I had realized how much of my childhood I had actually shared with him. Just like the incident with the window, a lot of it was things we had never spoken of afterwards.

I remembered the first time Daddy had failed to pick us up for our weekend visit with him. We were ten years old, and we had been waiting for him for hours. Since it was summer and we had no school, he was supposed to pick us up right after lunch that Friday. Mom had tried to call him repeatedly but got no answer. She had to call off work, because our babysitter already had plans for that evening. Connor got sick of waiting and said that he wanted to call Jake to come over. Mom asked me if I wanted to invite a friend too, but I said that I was going to ride my bike and took off out the door.

Daddy called late that night, and I picked up the phone in her room since she was in the bathroom. My father was drunk and slurring his words as he told me that he loved me more than anything in the world. Mom came into the room just as I was demanding to know why he hadn't shown up that day. She took the phone from me and told me to go back to bed. I saw Jake standing in the hallway, and Mom came out holding the phone.

"Go back to bed kids, please." She took the phone downstairs with her.

I waited until she disappeared from view and then sat down on the steps. Jake sat down beside me, and I could hear Mom talking in a hushed tone in the kitchen. I couldn't hear what she was saying, but I knew that she was just as upset as I was. Connor was either asleep, or he hadn't wanted to leave his room to find out what was happening.

Hot tears began to roll down my cheeks, and I couldn't stop them. Without saying a word, Jake put his arm around me, and I leaned into him and cried. We both scurried up the stairs when we heard Mom moving around in the kitchen. When she didn't immediately come upstairs, I walked over to Jake, who was standing in front of Connor's room, and I gave him a hug before returning to my room.

Thinking back on it now, I realized that Jake always seemed to be there for me. It was something that I had taken for granted until he removed himself from my life. I still saw him at school, but it wasn't the same. He wanted me to leave him alone until I made my final decision. It was that word final that made me realize how important this was to me. If I told him no this time, he would move on with his life without me. Maybe he would even get back with Madison.

I had seen her trying to flirt with him one day by his locker. He had looked decidedly uncomfortable as she placed her hand on his arm while she talked to him in a manner that disregarded his right to personal space. I had a good view of them from an advantageous angle around the corner. It had started with a desire to see him and had turned into spying when I saw Madison approach him. Jake said something to her and started to walk away. She had to hurry to keep up with his long-legged stride.

After what Jake had revealed to me about their first bedroom encounter, I viewed Madison's apology in a different light. She had just been fishing for information about my relationship with Jake. Why she would return with him to my bedroom after he called out my name while he was with her was something that made me mistrust her intensely. It seemed to me like she was playing a game, and I was her opponent. At least I was until I told her that Jake wasn't my boyfriend. She had then lost interest in me, because she hadn't spoken to me since.

I hadn't bothered to ask Kyle his opinion about Jake, since I already knew what he would say. He would ask me what I was waiting for. It took me three weeks to realize that Mom had been right. In my heart I had known all along what I wanted.

Kyle happened to be over my house doing homework with me when I made my decision. I had been looking at the same page of my history textbook for several minutes without reading a word. Jake and Connor were at their basketball game, and I wanted to go there immediately. Fortunately, it was a home game at our school.

Kyle was startled when I suddenly announced my intentions. "The game already started a while ago."

"I know, but I don't care. Will you drive me?" I asked as I stood up and left all my books on the kitchen table.

He drove me and asked me what was going on, but I told him not to break my concentration. I still hadn't worked out exactly what I would say to Jake, but I knew that I wanted to say it now. He was on the court playing the game when we arrived. Kyle followed me as I walked toward the sidelines and spotted Madison, who was a cheerleader.

"Hey, Madison." She looked at me in surprise as I approached her. "Last time we talked, I told you that Jake wasn't my boyfriend. He is now, so I would appreciate it if you would back off."

"Jake is your boyfriend!" Kyle exclaimed. "When did this happen?"

"It's about to happen now," I said right before the buzzer went off.

It was halftime, and Madison had to do her routine with the rest of the cheerleaders. Jake and Connor came over to see what Kyle and I were doing there.

I spoke before anyone else could say a word. "Hi, Jake. I decided that you're my boyfriend. I'm gonna go wait on the bleachers, and then I want to kiss you after the game is over."

Jake stared at me for a moment before a huge smile lit up his face. "The hell with that!"

I didn't have to wait until after the game for my kiss after all. Our team won the game too, but that didn't have anything to do with me.

Chapter 15

After Jake and I started dating, he wasn't allowed to sleep over anymore. This rule was put in place by my mom and his parents. Mom actually tried to have "the talk" with me.

"It's a little late for that, Mom." Maybe I should have phrased that differently.

"You've already had sex? I thought you just kissed a few times." She looked extremely upset.

"No, calm down. I just meant that I already learned about it in school." Little did she know that the only reason I hadn't had sex yet was because Jake had refused my advances.

Mom was relieved. "I know I should have talked to you about this sooner, but you seemed to have no interest in dating."

"I didn't," I confirmed.

"You're growing up, Cam, but you're still only seventeen. There's no need to rush into anything that you're not ready for. If Jake cares about you, he'll wait for you."

She had no idea how backwards she had it. Now that I thought about it, it was funny how reversed our roles had been. I had been the one pressuring Jake to have sex instead of the other way around. Somehow, I didn't think she would appreciate the humor in that. What she had said made me realize how much Jake cared about me. A lot of other guys had asked me out because they thought they could have casual sex with me.

"We just started dating, Mom. We're not even thinking about that yet." This was true in some ways. My attempts to have sex with Jake had been about trying to avoid a romantic relationship with him. Now I was in no hurry since we began dating.

A funny little laugh escaped from Mom. "You may not be thinking about it, but Jake most certainly has it on his mind. Don't get me wrong. I think he's a great guy, but he's still a teenage boy."

I was getting more uncomfortable with this conversation by the minute. Apparently, her mom radar didn't extend to the wayward thoughts of her teenage daughter. Since I wasn't about to confide how many times I had pictured Jake naked, from memory no less, I signaled that I was ready to drop this subject.

"Okay, Mom, I understand what you're saying. Nobody's going to talk me into anything I don't want to do." Those were the key words—don't want to do. I suddenly felt very guilty.

Mom seemed to understand the implications of my words, because she also became uneasy with our discussion. "I just want you to know that you can always talk to me if you have any questions or anything."

"Thanks, Mom. I will."

Jake and I were going out on real dates, just like any other couple. I had worn the jeans and top I bought for the party on our first date, which had been to a casual restaurant and to a movie after dinner. There had been lots of kissing in his car before we said goodnight. Connor seemed to be okay with our relationship, because it didn't intrude on his guy time with Jake. I still hung out with my own friends just like I always had.

Jason was the only one of my friends to confront me about Jake. "I heard that you and Jake are together."

"We are," I confirmed.

"So that's why you turned me down? Because you were with him? Why didn't you tell me?"

"It's complicated. Things were kind of shaky with us then," I explained.

"I guess that's why you went out with Dylan, to make him jealous. But you wouldn't do that to me, because we're friends." Jason smiled at me.

He had misunderstood the whole thing, but it seemed to make him feel better, so I didn't correct him. "Are we cool?"

"We're cool," he said, and he sounded like he meant it.

He sauntered away with a little wave, and I turned to see Madison watching me with a calculating look. "I guess I didn't give you enough credit, Cameron. I didn't think you knew how to play those kinds of games with guys. Enjoy it while it lasts. Pretty soon the novelty will wear off, and Jake will go looking for a real girl. Like me." She flounced away in her cute skirt.

"Do you have time to go shopping with me after school?" I asked Kyle at lunch.

"Who are you, and what did you do with Cam?" Kyle quipped.

"I'll explain it later," I said, since we weren't alone at our lunch table.

Madison had thrown down a challenge, and I was going to let her know that I was up for the fight. I had no fear that she had a chance with Jake, but I was going to show her that I could beat her at her own game. Kyle was thrilled with this new development. He had been ecstatic at the game when I announced that Jake was my boyfriend and as catty about Madison as any best friend would be.

"Did you see the look on her face?" Kyle had crowed. "She thought she had him wrapped around her finger until you showed up. It wiped that fake smile right off."

Now she had apparently bounced back from disappointment. I knew that her locker was in the same section where Jake's was located, and I was going to pay him a little visit in the morning. This time our shopping trip was actually kind of fun, because I was buying battle gear. While I was at it, I bought more jeans, bras, tops, and new pajamas. It was much easier to shop now that I knew what sizes I needed.

"My little girl is growing up." Kyle pretended to wipe tears from his eyes. "You should buy a few dresses in case Jake takes you somewhere fancy."

"Okay," I grumbled, and Kyle raised his eyebrows at my acquiescence. I wasn't about to dress girly all the time just because I had a boyfriend, but I had realized that my usual clothes might get me turned away from some places.

Connor gaped at me the next morning. "I guess I need to find another place to sleep tonight."

I rolled my eyes. "Not everything is about sex."

"That is." He gestured toward my outfit.

When I played a game, I played to win. I had on a bright red miniskirt and matching top. The color alone would draw attention to me, not to mention how much leg I was showing. I had worn my hair down, of course, and applied the red lipstick I had bought for the party. Even I hardly recognized myself when I looked in the mirror. I filled Connor in on why I was dressed like this while he drove us to school.

He got a good laugh out of it. "You're jealous!"

That was not the reaction I had expected. "What?"

"You're jealous of Madison, and you're fighting over Jake," he taunted.

"I'm not jealous of anyone. This is not about Jake. It's about Madison being a—"

Connor talked over me. "It's about showing Jake that you're hotter than Madison."

"No," I said in annoyance.

"Why don't you just admit it, Cam? You're finally acting like a real girl."

It irked me that he had used the same phrase as Madison. "I am a real girl, Connor. Get that through your male chauvinist head."

"Okay, okay," he relented. "Don't start lecturing me. I get enough of that at school."

Sometimes I wondered how his girlfriend put up with him. We went our separate ways when we arrived at school, and I headed straight for Jake's locker. He was putting his backpack away, and I saw Madison walking toward him.

"Hey, Jake," I called as I approached him.

"Hey, Ca—" He had started to speak as he was turning toward me, but he was apparently struck speechless by my appearance.

"Oh hey, Madison," I said as if I had just noticed that she was there.

Somebody behind me whistled. "Jake, my man. Who's this fine lady?"

I turned slightly as the guy walked up to us and recognized a boy from the basketball team.

"Hey, Tommy. This is my girlfriend, Cameron." Jake put a possessive arm around my waist.

"Holy shit! Cameron! I didn't even recognize you. You're Connor's sister."

"Yeah," I said. "It's nice to meet you, Tommy."

"It's very nice to meet you." He emphasized the word very.

"See you later," Jake said. "I've gotta walk Cam to her locker."

We left both Tommy and Madison staring after us. "Since when do you need to walk me to my locker?" I asked.

"Since you need a bodyguard to get through the halls. What the hell are you trying to do to me, Cam? I almost had a heart attack when I saw you." Jake was sending unfriendly glares at all the guys who were staring at me as we passed them.

"Madison said you would get tired of me." The words were out of my mouth before I realized what I was saying.

He pulled me to the side and stood looking into my eyes. "Damn it, Cam! I told you that I love you," he said, not caring who heard him. "Don't you believe me?"

I was flushing with pleasure and smiling at him like a fool. "I guess I forgot."

He leaned down to kiss me, and everyone around us clapped.

Kyle was suddenly there as we pulled back from our kiss. "That's my little girl. Look at her now, all grown up." He dabbed at his pretend tears. "I'm too emotional right now."

The warning bell rang then. "I have to get to my locker," I said. "See you later, guys." I hurried away from them so that I could get to class on time.

It was kind of fun to get so much attention, but I wouldn't want to deal with it on a daily basis. I didn't want to be aware of my appearance all the time. So, I put the miniskirt away at the end of the day. It would remain in my closet until a very special occasion in the future. I dressed in my usual clothes on most days, and saved my "girl" clothes for my dates with Jake.

I wore jeans and a feminine top when I went to his house for the first time. His parents already knew me from when they used to drop Jake off at our house before he could drive, but I hadn't met his brothers and sisters. One parent would always stay home with them instead of loading them all into the car, while the other drove Jake.

I loved being with his family. He had four sisters and one brother. I had heard so much about them over the years that I felt like I knew them. They ranged in age from thirteen to five, and they were all excited to meet me. I was soon surrounded by kids clamoring for my attention. Justin, the youngest, settled himself onto my lap with a book and asked me to read him a story.

"Justin," his mom admonished, "leave Cam alone."

"I don't mind," I said as the adorable little boy snuggled against me.

"Dinner will be ready soon," she said apologetically, but she smiled fondly at Justin.

I began to read his storybook, and the rest of the children listened quietly beside me. Jake had to sit on the chair across from me, because the rest of his siblings had squeezed themselves onto the couch with me. He had an affectionate smile on his face as he watched us. He was the only brunette in the family, and I guessed that his birth father must have had dark hair. His mother and the rest of his family were all blonde with blue eyes.

Jake had blue eyes too, but his were a different shade than the soft blue eyes of his siblings and dad. It was amazing how many different shades of blue there were, I thought as I noticed that his mother had yet another color of blue on the spectrum. Jake's eyes were the most noticeable of all in his family. They just caught a person's attention immediately. I decided that it must have been familiarity since childhood that had dulled my awareness of his beautiful eyes.

I observed all of this at the table during dinner with Jake's family. There was never a dull moment or a lapse in conversation. "Now you know why I stayed at your house for some peace and quiet," Jake told me as he drove me home.

"I was just thinking how boring it is at our house," I said.

"Only when I'm not around," he said with a laugh.

"You do make things more interesting," I agreed. "Pull over into that gas station."

"Do you need to use the restroom?" Jake asked as he parked the car.

"No, I just need to kiss you," I said before doing just that.

"You couldn't wait until we got to your house?" Jake asked and kissed me again before I could reply.

"It's your fault," I said when we broke for air. "You kept looking at me. Don't look at me if you don't want me to kiss you."

"When did I say that I don't want you to kiss me?"

Yes, we were that nauseating.

We had been dating for six months when Jake and I agreed that we were ready to have sex. It was a Friday night, and Mom was at work. Connor was out on a date with his girlfriend. I was more excited than nervous as I silently led Jake up to my room. We sat down on my bed, and our kissing quickly became heated. It wasn't until we took off our shirts, and he began to touch me through my bra as we kissed, that I began to feel like it wasn't right.

Jake pulled back and looked at me. "I know. We need to find our own place."

It was a strange time to realize it, but I knew in that moment that I loved him. He was attuned to my feelings, and he understood me so well. I had been thinking about the last time he had sex in this room, and he had somehow picked up on it. "I love you, Jake."

He kissed me passionately before he replied. "I love you, Cam. I don't know when it happened, but I've felt that way for a long time."

Our relationship had changed, but it was still the same in some ways. Jake and I were still here sharing our special moments alone. Sometimes the more things changed, the more they stayed the same.

He put his shirt back on. "C'mon, Cam. Pick your game. I'm gonna kick your ass."

"Keep dreaming, Jake." I put my shirt back on too.

We played video games, and Jake put up a good fight, but he couldn't beat me. "Just wait until I challenge you to a cooking competition!"

"I give up," I said.

"So, I'll be stuck doing all the cooking," he said with a laugh.

Something funny happened to my stomach when he so casually alluded to the future. It was what people called butterflies, but I was pretty sure it normally happened right before a kiss. Then again, I wasn't a normal girl.

We heard the front door open and the sound of someone giggling. Connor chased his girlfriend into the room, and they both skidded to a stop. "Oh, hi." Jen still looked uncomfortable in my presence. "Uh, goodnight."

"Goodnight," Jake and I called as they walked out of the room.

We heard the front door open, and Connor came back with a disappointed look on his face.

"You're playing video games? Couldn't you do that in the basement?"

"Remember when you told me not to touch your system?" I asked, enjoying his frustration. "You bought that with your own money. Blah, blah, blah."

"That was three years ago! You know seeing you ruins the mood for Jen," he complained.

"That's funny. Seeing Cam always puts me in the mood." Jake dropped the controller and shot out of the room before Connor could attack him. "Bye, Cam," he yelled as he made his escape from our house.

I was too busy laughing to answer. "The look on your face," I gasped and pointed at Connor.

He scowled at me. "I liked it better when you were avoiding each other."

I was still chuckling. "You walked right into that one. Anyway, if you must know. We haven't done anything. That's why we were playing video games instead of doing what you were planning to do with Jen."

"Oh." He looked mollified and embarrassed at the same time. "Uh, goodnight."

"Goodnight." It had been a very good night, I thought. I reflected on how scared I had been when Jake asked me out, but now I was glad that I had taken a chance on our relationship.

Chapter 16

More months passed without us finding another place to be alone. I didn't want my first time to be in a car, and on the couch felt too exposed with someone possibly being able to walk in on us. Jake told me not to worry about it and said that we had plenty of time for that in the future. We had fun going on dates and even just hanging out with his family.

I was starting to feel as comfortable at his house as he did at mine. Madison had also ceased to be a problem after she gave up on Jake and easily found a new boyfriend. Everyone at school now knew that Jake and I were a solid couple. Guys had stopped asking me out since it became clear that I wasn't interested in anyone else. I was happy and secure in my relationship with my boyfriend.

My eighteenth birthday was coming up, and Jake asked me what I wanted for my present. I was completely sure of my answer. "You," I said.

He smiled. "You already have me."

We were sitting in his car after our movie date, and I placed my hand on his thigh. "Not every part of you."

"I told you not to worry about that." Jake's light tone of voice had dropped an octave, however.

"I'm not worried. That's the whole point. It's not about proving anything or avoiding anything. I love you, Jake, but I also want you."

I had a plan for where we could go to be alone together. The banks seemed to know that my birthday was approaching too, because they had started sending me credit card offers. I had filled one out on a whim and been surprised to receive a credit card even though I didn't have a job.

Holding it in my hand had made me feel so grown up. My thoughts had turned to all the perks of being an adult, and I had realized that I could now go anywhere I wanted. That had led to the idea of getting a hotel room. I could use my new credit card to pay for a room.

Jake listened to me explain my plans. "Are you sure about this, Cam?"

"I'm absolutely sure. Do you still want to?" I didn't want to pressure him again.

His voice had dropped another octave. "If you move your hand a little higher, you'll have your answer."

"Or it might actually be a rock this time," I joked, but my voice wasn't quite steady. Instead of moving my hand higher, I took hold of his hand. "I'll get us a room that Friday after my birthday."

"It's not set in stone, Cam." He gave my hand a squeeze. "You can still change your mind anytime."

I didn't change my mind. Our birthday was on a Wednesday this time, and Mom took the day off and let us stay home from school like she did every year. The three of us spent the entire day together and went out for dinner. Connor and I had both opted not to have a party, but Jake's siblings threw us a "surprise" party on Thursday.

We heard them giggling, but we pretended to be surprised when they popped up from behind their couch. They were bursting with excitement as they led us into the kitchen where their parents had a cake for us. They had known Connor for years, and the kids treated him like another brother. I had made plans to hang out with my friends on Saturday, but Friday was for me and Jake. He got me a cool t-shirt and two tickets for a concert to see one of my favorite bands.

"Hmm," I said coyly. "I wonder who I should take with me."

"I wanna go!" Justin shouted.

"You're too little," Katie, who was fourteen, told him.

"Am not!" Justin glared at her. "I'm six," he added proudly.

"Cam doesn't want to go with you," ten-year-old Lexie said. "She wants to go with her boyfriend."

"I'm gonna be her boyfriend," Justin informed her. "We're gonna get married."

The others laughed at him while I bent down to kiss the top of his head. "I can't believe it," Jake said. "My own brother moving in on my girl."

"How about we go for ice cream instead?" I offered. "Just me and you on Sunday."

"Yeah, ice cream!" Justin stuck his tongue out at his sisters.

"We'll bring some home for you guys too." I didn't want them to feel bad by leaving them out.

"You don't have to do that, Cam," Jake's dad said.

"I want to. I'm not going to get to see them as much when I go away to college." This was our senior year of high school already.

It was hard to concentrate on my classes on Friday. As soon as we pulled into our driveway after school, I told Connor that I would be back soon.

"Where are you going?" Connor asked.

"I need to get something at the store," I lied.

"Pick me up some beer," he joked.

I had driven down the street and around the corner when I got a text message from Mom telling me to get a gallon of milk. Now I would really have to stop at the store. I drove to the hotel first and paid for a room. The credit card worked, and I received a key to the room.

"What'd you need at the store?" Connor asked when I returned home with the milk.

"It's in my purse." Let him think it was a feminine product for all I cared.

He probably did, because he looked away from my purse in distaste.

"Are you going out tonight?" Mom asked.

"Yes," we both answered.

"Don't forget you have to work in the morning," she reminded Connor.

She had been telling us since we were sixteen that she was cutting off our spending money once we turned eighteen. If we wanted to pay for fun, we would have to get jobs. She apparently meant it, because she had given us more money than usual for this birthday but reminded us that this was it until Christmas.

Connor had already gotten a job. He must have realized that he now needed to work in order to afford to take his girlfriend out. I still hadn't gotten around to looking for a job yet, mostly because Jake insisted on paying for all our dates. I suddenly wondered how his parents could afford to give him so much spending money when they had six kids.

"What time do you think you'll be home?" Connor asked me after I got out of the shower.

"Probably an hour before Mom comes home."

He looked at me suspiciously. "What's open that late? You can't get into the clubs yet."

"We're going to go driving around," I said.

He was still looking at me with suspicion. "Cam—"

I cut him off impatiently. "Since it was your birthday too, you know that I'm eighteen now. Which means that I'm an adult. Hence, it's none of your business."

"Forget it," he said. "I don't wanna know."

I went into my room to get dressed, and Connor went into the bathroom to take his own shower. It was warm outside, so I wore shorts and a t-shirt. I left my hair down for Jake, although I didn't think that would be his main focus tonight. Connor left before Jake arrived, and I suspected that he was going to pick up Jen and take advantage of having the house to himself. Jake greeted me with a brief kiss, and we were pretty quiet as he drove to the hotel. I told him that I already had the key, so we wouldn't need to waste time checking in.

"Do you want to go get something to eat first?" Jake sounded a little nervous too.

"I'm not hungry," I said as he parked the car. "Are you?"

When his eyes met mine, I saw the heat in his gaze. "Not for food."

He then opened his door and stepped out of the car, and I saw him open the door to the backseat as I exited the car. He took out a couple of bags, and I saw that one contained orange juice. "For my lady," he said with a smile.

"What's in the other one?" I asked.

"Snacks. You're going to need to get your energy back."

"Ha! I think you're the one who's going to need energy."
I was grateful that he was attempting to lighten the mood,
because the intensity between us had been almost too much. I
was nervous again as I unlocked the door to the room.

Jake set the bags down on the dresser and turned to look at
me. "If you change your mind, just tell me to stop. Okay,
Cam?"

"Yeah." I walked up to him and ran a hand up his arm.
"Did you bring the condom?"

"Yeah, it's in my pocket. Do you know that you're
corrupting a minor?" Jake teased.

His eighteenth birthday was two months away, and he had
taken to joking about me being the older woman.

"Ha! I think you're the one who's corrupting me."

"Not yet," he said. Then he leaned down to kiss me.

I was already in a heightened state of desire from thinking
about this every day for the past week, and his kiss inflamed me
further. My hands slipped under his shirt to touch his back, and I
reveled in the feel of his skin. He picked me up, and I wrapped
my legs around him as we continued to kiss. Jake walked with
me to the bed and set me down.

His eyes. God, the way he was looking at me! I could
barely remember how to breathe.

"Cam," he said, his voice coarse with passion. "Are you
sure?"

I yanked my shirt up and over my head, flinging it to the floor. "Get over here and corrupt me, Jake."

Chapter 17

I slept in on Saturday because I had gotten home so late. Mom was still sleeping, and Connor was presumably at his job. I stopped to look at myself in the bathroom mirror to see if I looked any different. Of course, my face still looked the same as it always did, except for the slight flush on my cheeks as I thought about what had happened last night.

Jake had made me feel things I'd never felt before, and my body had come alive with his touch. The experience was so much more than I had imagined it would be. The intimacy we had shared made me feel closer to him than I had ever felt to anyone else. I thought back to my original plan to have sex with him and go back to being just friends. Now I knew that it would have been a failure, because my desire for Jake hadn't gone away after we made love. In fact, it was already coming back as I thought about how it had felt to be with him.

There had been a happy, comfortable atmosphere between us afterwards as we drank juice, ate snacks, and talked. We snuggled while we watched some TV. I even dozed off for a while, and Jake woke me up when it was time to leave. He laughed at my dismay when I noticed the blood on the sheets.

"It's because you were a virgin, Cam."

"But the maids will see it," I fretted.

"We'll be long gone by then. It's probably not the first time they've seen something like that," he reasoned.

I was still embarrassed by it as I got dressed. "Let's get out of here."

"Hey." Jake stopped my flight toward the door. "Do you regret it?"

"I would have brought a towel or something if I knew that was going to happen." My thoughts were still on the stained sheets.

"That's not what I meant, Cam. Do you regret what happened between us?"

I was startled by his question. "No. Do you?"

"No, as long as you're okay with it. This has been the best night of my life. I know it wasn't as good for you, but it'll be better next time."

"It gets better than that?" I asked in wonder.

Some of the heat came back into his eyes as he looked at me. "Yes, Cam. I promise to make it better next time."

I suddenly didn't want to leave this room, but I knew that I had to get home before Mom returned.
"It's time to go," I said reluctantly.

When we were in the car on the way home, I continued the conversation. "Why did you say that it wasn't as good for me?"

"From what I've been reading, the first time isn't that good for girls," Jake said.

"You've been reading about sex? I thought you already knew about it from experience." I was torn between being curious about his sexual past and dreading the answer.

"I don't know much," he admitted to my surprise. "My first time was at a party, and I was drunk, so my memory of it isn't that clear. It was weird to wake up in her bed the next morning since we weren't even dating. Then she kept hanging on me and trying to get with me again. I thought I might as well since we already did it before anyway. It was even worse that time, because I ended up calling out your name. She was pissed, and I thought that was it, but then she was all over me again in a few days."

"You mean you've only been with Madison?" I asked.

"Yeah, three times. It wasn't exactly a great learning experience. That's why I've been reading up on the female response to try to make it good for you."

This struck me as funny. "You've been studying how to have sex with me?"

"Yeah," he grinned. "I didn't mind doing homework for once." Then he sounded uncertain. "How'd I do?"

"It was good," I told him. There had been the pain at the end, but it had been amazing before that.

"It'll be better next time," he insisted.

Jake drove me home, and we kissed goodnight. There was a text message from him on my phone when I woke up. He had written that he loved me. I texted him back that I loved him too.

Then I decided to make breakfast for Mom. I cooked the bacon first, and then I made the eggs when I heard Mom walking around upstairs. She walked into the kitchen just as the toast was done.

"Wow, it's not even my birthday," she said with a smile.

I set her toast down beside her plate of eggs. "It doesn't have to be your birthday for me to show you how much I appreciate you."

"I'm still not giving you anymore spending money." She tried to keep her voice stern, but she ruined it by laughing.

I walked up to her and gave her a hug. "I mean it, Mom. I love you."

She was startled by my fierce tone of voice. "I love you too, Cam." She pulled back to look at me. "Is everything okay?"

I didn't know why I was suddenly so emotional. "Yeah, it's just that you've always been there for us when Daddy wasn't. I just want you to know how much that means to me."

Mom's eyes were glistening with tears. "Oh sweetheart! You're my wonderful baby girl," she said as she hugged me.

It was all coming to an end, I realized. This was my last year of high school before I left home for college. I blinked back my own tears. "Eat your breakfast before it gets cold." I sat down at the table and ate with her.

She asked about my plans for the day, and I told her that I was going to hang out with my friends. "I'm going to start looking for a job next week."

"It's good to get some work experience before college. I think it'll help you focus on your goals if you know what it's like to work for your money. Too many kids fail their classes in college, because all they did was party," Mom said.

"I'm not into that at all." I could never understand the appeal of getting wasted. For me nothing could compare to the adrenaline rush of playing sports. At least nothing could compare to it until last night, I thought.

"I know, and I hope that won't change." What she left unspoken was her fear that Connor or I would become alcoholics like our father.

"So, what are you doing tonight? Do you have a date?" I asked in order to lead the conversation away from uncomfortable topics.

"I do, and Nathan wants to go to this ridiculously expensive restaurant. I can't see the sense in spending so much on one meal." She shook her head at this foolishness.

"He's paying, right?" I smiled when she nodded. "Then just enjoy yourself. You don't go to fancy places all the time. Let him splurge if he wants to."

"I guess it'll be nice to dress up for a change," she conceded.

Since she worked in a factory, Mom wore mostly casual clothes all the time. That seemed like a bonus to me, but I had to admit that she looked beautiful in her dark blue dress. I saw the adoring way that Nathan looked at her, and I hoped that this relationship would last. He had been around for a while, and Connor and I both liked him, but I hadn't dropped my guard and allowed myself to get attached to him.

Before I witnessed the romantic scene when Nathan came to pick Mom up for dinner, she and Kyle had been there to see me get a delivery of a dozen red roses. Connor had just gotten home from work and gone up to his room when the doorbell rang. Kyle and I were playing a video game before we went to meet up with the rest of the guys. Mom answered the door and called out that it was for me. Kyle followed me to see who was at the door. A delivery man handed the flowers to me, and both Mom and Kyle stood where they could read the card in my hand.

Cam,
All my love always,
  Jake

I wasn't the type to daydream about romantic gestures, but I felt incredibly happy right then. He had talked about next time last night, but his note said so much more. Jake had alluded to our future before, but here it was clearly spelled out that he was talking about more than just the near future. It was something that I hadn't yet given any thought to as I lived our relationship from week to week.

"That boy is so romantic," Mom sighed. "It's so rare these days in somebody so young."

Kyle was unusually quiet about it until we left my house. "You had sex with Jake!"

I tried to keep a poker face. "What gives you that idea?"

"You're blushing right now, and you never blush. You also blushed when you were reading that card. He's romantic enough to send you flowers afterward too. I'm so jealous! How could you not tell me about it right away?"

"Some things are private, Kyle." I had never felt shy about talking to him about anything before.

"I know that, Cam. I'm not asking for details, but you could have just told me that it happened."

"It happened," I confirmed.

"Did I mention that I'm jealous?"

I smiled. "There's a lot to be jealous about."

"A lot, huh? I knew it. With him being that tall, other parts of him are likely to be large too." Kyle took his eyes off the road to smirk at me.

It must be my day for blushing, because my cheeks were on fire. "I didn't mean it like that!"

He was laughing, and I knew that he was just teasing, but I was embarrassed for probably the first time in our friendship. I had been naïve to think that having sex would have no effect on me, and I soon found that it was impossible for me to go back to the way I was before.

It had never occurred to me that kissing wouldn't be enough anymore. Our relationship had been altered once we crossed that line, and sexual tension was always simmering between us now. Even with school, my soccer games, and my part-time job, I still felt restless.

Jake, I soon noticed, was avoiding spending time alone with me. We had often just hung out at my house and watched a movie on TV, but now he made sure that all our dates were in public. Our kissing sessions in his car were also much shorter than they had been before. Things went on this way for several weeks as my passion for him became like a fever raging through my body.

Mom had gone on a date with her fiancé. Yes, Nathan had proposed to her when he took her to that fancy restaurant. I saw how happy she was, and I was thrilled for her. Connor was actually working that Saturday night. Jake was taking me out to a movie, and he hesitated when I told him to come in for a minute.

"I want to show you something," I said.

"Okay, but we need to leave soon if we want to get there in time." He followed me upstairs to my room. "What do you want to show me?"

"How much I've missed you." I ran a hand over his chest. "Have you missed me, Jake?" I asked in a flirty voice I'd never used before.

"Cam," he protested, but his gaze was becoming heated with desire.

"I'm over it," I said as I pressed myself against his body. "We'll make this room our place."

Jake groaned with pent up passion and leaned down to give me a hungry kiss. Half our clothes were on the floor within minutes. "Do you have anything with you?" I asked while I was still able to think.

"No, but I know where Connor keeps his condoms." He went to get one and returned to find me completely naked. "I guess I don't have to ask if you're sure."

We never did make it to the movie.

Chapter 18

"I'm getting my own place," Jake said. He had insisted on driving me home after his birthday party even though I had come there with Connor.

"How?" I asked. "You don't even have a job."

"Remember when you saw me at the cemetery, and I told you about my first dad and grandpa?"

"Yeah." I was looking at him, but he kept his eyes on the road.

"Well, they left me some money."

The atmosphere in the car had changed. Jake sounded very uncomfortable talking about this even though he was the one who brought it up. "That's great, but don't you think you should save it to help pay for college?" I sounded like my mother.

"There's enough for college too. It was set up in a trust fund." He still wasn't looking at me as he hurried on. "I got the first part when I turned sixteen and the second now for my eighteenth birthday. There are, uh, two more payments. The next one is when I turn twenty-one, and I'll get the rest when I'm thirty."

It was dawning on me what he was saying. I didn't know much about trust funds, but I knew it was something rich people had. Jake didn't just get some money. He must have a sizable inheritance if it was split up into so many parts. "Your car," I said, and he understood what I meant.

"Yeah, there was no way my parents would have been able to afford to buy me a car. Mom told me about the trust fund right before my sixteenth birthday. She said that it was my money, but she hoped that I wouldn't blow it all. I remembered my grandpa talking about me driving him around one day, and I knew he'd want me to have a car." He smiled with the memory. "I wish I could have taken him for that ride." He cleared his throat. "Anyway, I put the rest in the bank."

I didn't know how to feel about this revelation. "No wonder you always have money to pay for dates and stuff. Does Connor know about this?"

"He knows about my first dad and my grandpa, but not about the money. Please don't tell anyone, Cam. I don't want people to treat me differently."

"I won't," I promised. It was too much to take in all at once, so I focused on his immediate plans. "Aren't your parents upset about you moving out? You haven't even finished high school yet."

"They trust me to be responsible, but they wouldn't be able to stop me anyway since I'm eighteen. It's not like I'm moving far away, and I'll still see them more than when I'm away at college." He laughed. "Katie can't wait, because she'll have her own room."

We had just left his house, and his family had happily celebrated his birthday. Nobody seemed to be upset with him, so I guess they were okay with it. I still felt like it was my fault he was moving out. "Jake, I know it's frustrating sometimes when we can't be alone, but you don't have to move out of your house."

"I won't lie to you, Cam. Knowing that we can be together without worrying about someone walking in on us is part of the reason I want my own place, but it really is crowded at my house. Like I said, Katie will be able to have her own room now."

I couldn't deny that I was excited about the thought of truly being able to be alone with him in a place where no parents or siblings could come home unexpectedly. We'd had a close call the other day when Mom arrived home early from work. Some machine had broken down, and they had sent her shift home. Fortunately, Jake and I still had our clothes on, but she had seen us walk out of my room together. This had earned me another talk with her the following day, this time about contraception. She had insisted on setting up an appointment for me with a gynecologist.

"You can ask her questions that you might not feel comfortable asking me." Mom had been open and nonjudgmental, but I still didn't want to discuss my sex life with her.

"Did you have this talk with Connor?" I wondered aloud.

She smiled ruefully. "Yeah, years ago, and he was even more embarrassed than you are. I made sure that he knew about condoms by demonstrating how to put one on a cucumber."

The visual was so hilarious that I laughed until I was almost crying, and Mom cracked up too. "He hasn't eaten cucumbers since," she said, wiping tears from her eyes.

"Stop," I cried, still laughing. "I'll be scarred for life. Poor Connor."

She laughed a little longer, then became serious again. "That was a talk that your father should have had with him, but I did the best I could. Realistically, with me working the hours that I work, I knew that it would be a big temptation for him no matter what I said about waiting. That's why it was a relief not to have to worry about that with you until now."

"I know about safe sex." That was as far as I would go to acknowledge my involvement in this subject.

"There is no such thing as safe sex. Not really. No method is a hundred percent safe. Accidents happen, and I want you to come to me if you're ever in that situation. You don't have to deal with it on your own."

I may not have the best dad, but I was blessed with a terrific mom. "Thanks, Mom."

Her expression was fierce with maternal love. "I mean it, Cam. Even after Nathan and I are married, you can still turn to me for help. He understands how important you and Connor are to me."

It was reassuring to hear her say that. I was going to miss her when I left for college, and I was glad that Nathan would be with her. They were getting married in June, but he wasn't moving in until then. He lived in an apartment, so it made more sense for him to move.

I hadn't told Mom about Jake getting his own place, because her sex talk hadn't seemed like the appropriate time to mention it. His parents were going to help him search for an apartment, so they seemed to have no problem accepting the fact that he was moving out. I had thought about what he had told me about his inheritance and decided that it didn't concern me. That was his money and his business, and I didn't really care to know any more about it.

It only took Jake two weeks to find an apartment, and he bought all new furniture. "I can take it with me when I go to college."

"I don't think it will all fit in a dorm," I said.

"I'm going to get an apartment," he told me.

"Where do you think you'll go?" My back was turned to him as I asked that question.

"That depends on where you go. I applied to all the same schools that you did."

I turned to look at him. "How do you know which schools I applied to?"

"I asked your mom. We had a pretty long conversation about it. She doesn't think that we should live together until we finish college, but she knows that'll be your decision."

The butterflies in my stomach were having a field day. "You want me to live with you at college?"

"If you're ready for that," Jake said. "If not, then we'll wait. You don't have to decide right now." He suddenly looked uncertain. "You don't mind if I go to the same college, do you?"

"I was hoping you would, but I didn't want to be clingy," I admitted.

He laughed. "I'm trying not to be clingy either, because I know how independent you are, but I wouldn't be able to stand being away from you for that long."

I hugged him. "I don't want to be away from you either." I pulled back to look at him. "So, this will be your first night sleeping in your apartment?"

"Yeah," he confirmed. "It's so quiet compared to home."

I ran my hand over his chest and watched what it did to his eyes. "Have you tried out your new bed yet?"

"You have a one-track mind," he scolded, but his voice betrayed him.

"Only when it comes to you," I said before he leaned down to kiss me.

His bed was comfortable, but I was soon too distracted to care about that. It was Monday, and Jake and I planned our next date for Saturday evening. He wanted to go to an expensive restaurant, but I told him that I didn't feel like dressing up, and that we should postpone that for another time.

"Okay, how about we eat somewhere casual and go to a movie?" Jake asked.

"That sounds good," I agreed, but I had my own secret plans for that evening.

Jen had recently gotten her own car, so I told Connor that I was taking our car. "Why?" Connor asked. "Jake's got his own car."

"So does Jen. You've been hogging our car forever, and I haven't complained. I want to drive tonight, so deal with it." The reason for this was because I didn't want Jake to see me until I arrived at his apartment.

Connor relented after he called Jen, and she agreed to drive him on their date. Fortunately, she picked him up before I was ready to leave. I had called Jake to tell him that I was driving, and he had been surprised. "I have a birthday present for you," I said.

"My birthday was three weeks ago, and you already gave me my present."

"Not all of it," I said mysteriously. "I'm bringing the rest of it over later."

"What is it?" Good, he was curious.

"It's a surprise." I was sure he would like it.

As I drove to his apartment, I remembered how I had thought that I could just have casual sex with Jake and walk away. Now I knew that there was nothing casual about this. My feelings for him, both emotional and sexual, were more intense than I had ever imagined they could be. No wonder I had been scared of being in a relationship, because the emotions were so strong that severing our bond would cut deep. I was too far into it to be able to turn back now however. Once I parked the car, all my thoughts turned to seeing Jake and what his reaction would be.

He didn't disappoint me when he opened the door. His blue eyes traveled slowly from my face to my feet before he stepped back to allow me to enter. I was wearing the red miniskirt and top I had worn to school after Madison told me that Jake would return to her. That seemed like ages ago, but I remembered that Jake had been struck speechless by my appearance.

He needed no words now either as he closed the door and pulled me up against it while I wrapped my legs around him. His searing kiss told me how much he liked his present. When his lips pulled back from mine, it was only so that he could see to walk to his bedroom. He stopped several times to kiss me along the way. I kicked my shoes off after he set me down on his bed.

He stood looking at me. "You're beautiful."

I leaned back in what I hoped was a sexy pose and gazed up at him. "You're hot."

Jake joined me on the bed and kissed me while his hand moved up my bare thigh. His fingers teasingly caressed my skin as he broke off the kiss to speak to me in a low voice. "I dreamed about you that night, about touching you like this."

I moaned as his hand moved up to make contact with my panties.

He stopped. "What are you wearing?" His voice sounded even rougher now. He pulled my miniskirt up to reveal silky red panties. His eyes were burning with lust as he removed my top in one swift movement.

I had on a matching silky red bra that I had bought during my first ever shopping trip to Victoria's Secret. The thongs had looked extremely uncomfortable, so I had bypassed them in favor of the panties, which were still sexier than my regular cotton ones. Jake sure seemed to like them, but they eventually ended up on his floor.

We lay cuddling in contentment after our passionate lovemaking. "Hey," Jake suddenly said. "Where's my present?"

I smacked his arm. "If you didn't like it, I'll get you a pair of socks next time."

"As long as you're wearing them—and nothing else." His hand skimmed over my thigh.

"Later," I said. "Right now, I'm hungry. Get dressed and take me out to eat."

"You're so demanding." He pretended to be annoyed.

"You love it," I said as I sat up.

He pulled me back and kissed me. "I love you, Cam."

I smiled, feeling completely happy. "I love you, Jake."

We went out to eat, but we decided to skip the movie and go back to his apartment. I took the miniskirt with me when I left for college. I had received a soccer scholarship that paid for everything, so I lived in a dorm with a roommate. All my weekends were spent at Jake's apartment, however, and my roommate loved it. She had a new boyfriend she had met during her first day at college.

Sadly, Connor and Jen broke up after they went to different colleges. Kyle and Scott lasted another year before their relationship ended for good this time. "We both changed," Kyle told me. He seemed to be dealing with it better than last time, probably because it had been mutual this time.

"Most high school romances don't last," Jake said when I told him the news. "People change as they grow up, and they want different things."

This worried me. "What about us?"

"I think we're going to beat the odds. We've grown up together, and I've loved you through all your changes." He smiled at me. "We've got more places to go together. We haven't even been to Texas yet."

We continued to go through changes, but we stayed together. I made new friends, even with a few girls on my soccer team, and I lost touch with most of my old friends. The only one I was still close to was Kyle. He even stayed at Jake's apartment when he came to visit me. I think that's when I truly began to believe that we would make it. Life changes, but some things remain. Looking back, the constants for me have always been my family, Kyle, and Jake.

They are all here now to celebrate our marriage. Jake's family is now my family too. Justin is now eleven years old and has long since forgotten his vow to marry me. Katie is nineteen and in college, while we graduated a year ago. Jake is paying the tuition for all his siblings to go to college. Now that we're married, I suppose I'll find out all the details of his finances. It still doesn't concern me, because I earn my own money.

Kyle is here with his new boyfriend, Ethan. It's great to see him looking so happy again. "Where are you going on your honeymoon?" Ethan asks.

"Texas," Jake replies.

"That's an unusual choice," Nathan says. He took Mom to the Bahamas for their honeymoon.

Jake and I smile at each other, and I answer for both of us. "Texas is only the beginning."